CHRISTMAS CONTRACT FOR HIS CINDERELLA

CHRISTMAS CONTRACT FOR HIS CINDERELLA

JANE PORTER

MILLS & BOON

First published in Great Britain 2019
by Mills & Boon, an imprint of HarperCollins*Publishers*
1 London Bridge Street, London, SE1 9GF

Large Print edition 2020

© 2019 Jane Porter

ISBN: 978-0-263-08439-9

Printed and bound in Great Britain
by CPI Group (UK) Ltd, Croydon, CR0 4YY

CHAPTER ONE

MONET WILDE WAS in the back room on the fifth floor of Bernard Department Store, searching for a customer's missing gown, which she was sure had gone to alterations but apparently had never actually arrived there, when one of her salesgirls appeared, informing her that a gentleman was waiting for her, and while he was brusque, he was not as irritable as Mrs. Wilkerson, who couldn't understand how her daughter's bridal gown could just disappear.

Monet sighed and reached up to smooth a dark tendril that had come loose from her neat chignon, aware that she dressed more matronly than most matrons, but as the manager of the bridal department it was important to maintain a sense of decorum. "Did he say what he wants?" she asked with a glance at the clock on the stockroom wall. Fifteen minutes until closing. Fifteen minutes to find a very expensive gown for a very irate mother of the bride.

"You." The salesgirl's expression turned rueful. "Well, he asked for you. By name."

Monet's heart fell. "Tell me we haven't misplaced another gown."

"He didn't say. He just asked for you."

Monet's frown deepened. It had been a maddeningly busy day at Bernard's, the kind of busy that characterized Christmas shopping on a weekend in December. The customers had descended in hordes the moment the department-store doors opened this morning at nine, and the queues and demands had been endless. Apparently everyone had decided that an impromptu wedding was in order, and what could be more festive than getting married on Christmas, or a destination wedding for New Year's? Monet had spent hours already on the phone calling designers, other stores, seamstresses, trying to find out what was available, and what could be done with gowns that might be available, and she still had a dozen things to do before closing.

"Does he have a name?" Monet asked.

"Marcus Oberto, or something like that. He's Italian."

Monet froze, even as she silently corrected

the girl. Marcu Uberto was the name, and Marcu wasn't Italian, but Sicilian.

"I told him you were quite busy," the girl added. "But he said he'd wait. He said to take your time and there was no rush."

Monet didn't believe that for a second. Marcu was not a man to be kept waiting.

And yet what was he doing here? And why now?

Those two questions circled her brain, creating unwanted anxiety. She hadn't seen Marcu in eight years, and the last time she'd heard from him had been almost three years ago to the day. What could he possibly want this close to Christmas?

"Shall I give him a message?" the salesgirl asked with a cheeky smile. "I don't mind. He's seriously sexy. But then I adore Italians, don't you?"

Sicilian, Monet again silently corrected.

Marcu was Sicilian to the bone.

"Thank you for the offer," Monet said, "but I'll need to handle Signor Uberto. However, you could help me by phoning Mrs. Wilkerson and let her know we haven't forgotten her, and we should have news about the missing bridal gown first thing in the morning."

"Will we?" the girl replied, wrinkling her brow.

Monet couldn't even imagine the fallout if they didn't have good news. "We had better," Monet said firmly, squaring her shoulders and heading from the stockroom to face Marcu.

She spotted him immediately as she emerged through the silver-and-gray curtains. He stood in the center of the marbled floor, commanding the space, which was something since the fifth floor of Bernard's was topped by a glass dome and there was nothing but airy space on the bridal floor.

Tall, and broad through the shoulders, Marcu looked every inch the powerful wealthy aristocrat. Sophisticated and impeccably dressed in a charcoal suit and crisp white shirt—a suit and shirt she was certain from the tailoring had been made just for him. He'd paired the severe suit with a brilliant blue tie to set off his glossy black hair and piercing blue eyes. Eight years ago he'd worn his thick black hair long, but now it was cropped short and combed severely back from his brow while a hint of a shadow darkened his strong, angled jaw.

Monet's pulse pounded, and her mouth dried as she fought back a wave of memories—memories she couldn't bear to deal with on a night like this. Fortunately, he hadn't yet seen her, and she was grateful for small mercies as she fought to control her breathing, and center herself. She'd worked so hard to block the past that she felt wildly unprepared for dealing with Marcu Uberto in her present.

"Courage and calm," she whispered to herself. *"You can do this."*

"Marcu," she said politely, approaching him. "What brings you to Bernard's? Is there a gift, or purchase I can help you with?"

Monet. A streak of icy hot sensation raced through him at the sudden sound of her voice, a voice he'd know anywhere. It wasn't low or high, but there was a warmth to her tone, a sweetness, that matched her warm, sweet personality.

He turned to face her, half expecting the girl he'd last seen—petite, laughing, unassuming—but that wasn't the woman before him. The Monet he'd known in Palermo had a quick smile and bright golden-brown eyes, but this Monet was incredibly slender with a guarded gaze and firm full lips that looked as if they rarely smiled. She certainly wasn't smiling now, and with her hair drawn back, and dressed in a matronly lavender and gray tweed knit sheath dress with a matching knit jacket, she looked older than her twenty-six years.

"Hello, Monet," he said, moving forward to kiss her on each cheek.

She barely tolerated his cheek grazing hers before stepping quickly away. "Marcu," she replied quietly, unemotionally.

No, she wasn't happy to see him in her workspace, but then he hadn't expected her to welcome him with open arms.

"I've come to see you on a personal matter," he said, matching her detached tone. "I'd hoped that by coming here near to closing time, I would be able to steal you away afterward so we could talk without distractions."

Her already guarded expression shuttered completely, leaving her pretty features utterly blank. Once he'd known her so well that he could read all of her thoughts. He could read nothing now.

"The store might be closing soon," she answered with a small, stiff smile, "but unfortunately I'll be here for another hour. I still have orders to process and missing items to be found. Perhaps next time you're in London—with advance notice—we could have that visit?"

"The last time I was in London you refused to see me."

"Our schedules prevented it."

"No, Monet, *you* prevented it." His eyes met hers and held. "I won't be put off this time. I'm here, and happy to wait until you've finished."

"You won't be allowed to remain in the building after we close."

"Then I'll wait in my car." He glanced around the floor with its sleek silver Christmas trees and elegant decorations. "But why will it take you an hour to wrap things up? There's no one here. Everyone but your colleague has gone."

"I'm the manager and this is my department, so it falls to me to take care of all the pieces." She paused, her gaze lifting to meet his. "Surely you don't really want me to explain all the details of my job to you? I can't imagine you're that interested in bridal retail."

"I'm not surprised you opened and closed."

"It was an unusual day. We're short-staffed." She hesitated. "How did you know I opened?"

"I was here this morning. You were extremely busy so I left, and returned four hours ago. You were also very busy then, so here I am now."

She'd held his gaze the entire time, and while her features remained neutral, her brown eyes burned with intensity. "Has something happened?" she asked, her husky voice dropping even lower.

"There has been no accident, no tragedy."

"I don't understand then why you're here."

"I need your help."

"Mine?"

"Yes. You might recall that you owe me, and I've come to collect on that favor."

She seemed to stop breathing then, and he watched the heat fade from her eyes until they were glacier-cool. "I have much to do tonight, Marcu. This is not a good night."

He gestured to the pair of charcoal velvet armchairs near the platform and the tall trio of gilt-framed mirrors. "Would it be easier to just speak now?"

He saw her indecision and then she gave a curt nod. "Yes. Fine. Let's talk now," she said before walking to the chairs and sitting down on the edge of one, ankles crossing neatly under the chair.

Monet's heart hammered as Marcu followed her to the chairs backed by huge framed mirrors, and then took his time sitting down. The trio of mirrors gave her views of him from all angles as he first unbuttoned his dark jacket, and then sat down, all fluid grace and strength, before adjusting the cuff of his shirt, making sure it fit just so.

This was her workplace, and her floor, and yet he managed to make her feel as if she was the outsider...the imposter. Just as she'd been as a girl, living in the Uberto palazzo, supported by his father. Monet hated remembering. She hated being dependent on anyone. And she very much resented Marcu's appearance and reminder that she owed him.

She did owe him, too.

Years ago Marcu had come to her aid, providing an airline ticket and a loan when she needed to escape a difficult situation. He must have known there would be questions, and consequences, but he'd bought the airline ticket to London for her, anyway, and sent her with cash in her pocket, allowing her to escape Palermo, which is where the Uberto family lived, as did Monet's mother, who was Marcu's father's mistress.

Marcu had warned her as he'd dropped her off at the airport in Palermo that one day he would call in the favor. Monet was so desperate to escape that she'd blindly agreed. It had been eight years since that flight out of Palermo. It had been eight years since Marcu had told her that one day he would settle the score. It seemed that day was now. He had finally called in the favor.

"I need you for the next four weeks," he said, extending long legs. "I know you were once a nanny, and you were always good with my brother and sisters. Now I need you to take care of my three."

She hadn't heard from him in years. She'd avoided all mention of the aristocratic Sicilian Uberto family in years, the Uberto palazzo was one of the oldest and most luxurious in Palermo, and yet now he was here, asking her to drop everything to take care of his children. It would be laughable if it had been anyone else making such demands, but this was Marcu and that changed everything.

Monet drew a quick breath and shaped her smile, wanting to appear sympathetic. "As much as I'd like to help you, I really can't. This is a terrible time for me to take leave from my work here, as retail depends on Christmas, and then there are my own clients. I'm quite protective of my anxious Christmas and New Year's brides."

"I'm more protective of my children."

"As you should be, but you're asking the impossible of me. I won't be permitted to take any leave now."

"Then give notice."

"I can't do that. I love my work here, and I've fought hard for this position."

"I need you."

"You don't need *me*. You need a caregiver, a professional nanny. Hire a proper, skilled childminder. There are dozens of agencies that cater to exclusive clientele—"

"I will not trust my children with just anyone. But I will trust them with you."

She wasn't flattered. The very last thing she wanted to do was to take care of Marcu's children. She and Marcu had not parted on good terms. Yes, he'd helped finance her escape from Palermo, but *he* was the reason she'd had to leave Sicily in the first place. He'd broken her eighteen-year-old heart, and shattered her confidence. It had taken her years to build up her self-esteem again.

"I appreciate the vote of confidence," she retorted calmly. "But I can't leave Bernard's at this time of year. I have an entire department that depends on me."

"I'm calling in my favor."

"Marcu."

He simply looked at her, saying no more, but then, nothing else needed to be said on his part. They both knew she had agreed to return the favor. It was the only condition he'd made when he'd helped her leave Palermo. That one day he'd call in the favor, and when he did, she needed to help, and she'd agreed. As the years passed, Monet had come to hope—believe—that he would never need her. She'd hoped—believed—that he was so successful and comfortable that he'd forget the promise he'd extracted from her as he drove her to the airport. She'd grown so hopeful that he'd forgotten, that she herself had almost forgotten, that such a promise had even been made.

But clearly he hadn't, and that's all that mattered now. "This is not a good time to call in the favor," she murmured huskily.

"I wouldn't be here if it was a good time."

She looked away, brow knitting as she looked toward the huge Palladian-style window that dominated the fifth floor, adding to the department's restrained elegance. A few fat white flakes seemed to be floating past the glass. It wasn't snowing, was it?

"I promise to put in a good word with Charles Bernard," Marcu added. "I know him quite well, and I'm confident he will hold your position for you, and if not, I promise to help you find another job in January, after the wedding."

The wedding?

That caught her attention and she turned from the window and the snow to look at Marcu. His blue gaze met hers and held.

Marcu was still Marcu—brilliant, confident, arrogant, self-contained—and for a moment she was that eighteen-year-old girl again, desperate to be in his arms, in his life, in his heart. And then she collected herself, reminding herself that she wasn't eighteen; years had passed and thankfully they weren't the same people. At least, she wasn't the same girl. She wasn't attracted to him. She felt nothing for him.

So why the sudden frisson of awareness shooting through her, warming her from the inside out?

"I'm afraid you lost me," she said huskily. "What wedding?"

"Mine." He hesitated for a moment, then added, "Perhaps you didn't know that my wife died shortly after my youngest was born."

Monet had known, but she'd blocked that from her mind, too.

"I'm sorry," she said, fixing her gaze on the sharp knot of his blue tie, the silk gleaming in the soft overhead light. Of course he was exquisitely tailored. Marcu looked sleek and polished, Italian style and sophistication personified. Perhaps if she kept her attention fixed to the crisp white points of his collar, and the smooth lapels of his jacket, she could keep from seeing the face she'd once loved. It had taken her forever to get over him, and she would not allow herself to feel any attraction, or interest, or concern or affection.

"I need help with the children until after the wedding, and then it will get easier," he said. "I won't need your assistance longer than four weeks. Five, if it's really rough going."

Four or five weeks, working with him? Minding his children while he married again? "Does that include the honeymoon?" she asked drily.

He shrugged. "I have a conference mid-January in Singapore. I'm speaking so it depends on Vittoria if she'd like to make that our honeymoon."

Monet was appalled but it was none of her business. She wasn't going to get involved. "I can't do it. I'm sorry, but I've already paid you back the cost of the airline ticket, and the cash you lent me, with interest. Our debt should be settled."

"The debt is settled, the favor is not."

"They are one and the same."

"No, they are not one and the same. You do not owe me financially, but you owe me for the position you put me in when you left the palazzo, and the speculation you created by abruptly departing without saying goodbye to your mother, my father, my brother and sisters. You put me in a most difficult position, and that is the score that is to be settled now as once again I am in a difficult position and this time you *can* help me."

It crossed her mind that she could argue this point forever with him, but he would never change his stance. Marcu was fixed. He was absolutely immovable. Even at twenty-five he'd been mentally strong, physically strong, a force to be reckoned with. Perhaps that had been his appeal. Monet had been raised by a woman who couldn't put down permanent roots, and didn't know how to make a home, or even make responsible decisions. Monet's mother, Candie, was impulsive and irrational. Marcu was the opposite. He was analytical, cautious, risk-averse. He was reason personified.

The only time he'd ever surprised her was the night he'd kissed her, and made love to her, only stopping short of taking her virginity. And then his regret, and his scorn, had scarred her. In mere minutes he'd gone from passionate and sensual, to callous and cold.

Monet had left less than fourteen hours later, flying out of Palermo with nothing but the smallest knapsack of clothing. She owned very little. She and her mother had lived off the generosity of Marcu's father and Monet was not about to take any of the gifts he'd bestowed on her.

It proved easy to leave Palermo, and yet once she'd arrived in London, far too hard to forget Palermo. Not because she missed her mother, but Monet missed everything else—the busy life at the historic sprawling palazzo, Marcu's younger brother and sisters, and then there was Marcu himself…

In that first year in London Monet spent far too many nights sleepless, agonizing over the evening in Marcu's arms. It hurt to remember his kisses and his touch, and yet they were the most potent, powerful emotions and sensations she had ever felt. She had felt like a flame—flickering, hot, radiant. He had woken something inside of her that she hadn't known existed. And his harsh rejection of her had been confusing…shattering.

She'd worked to forget Sicily. She'd tried to put the entire Uberto family from her mind, and yet she missed the children. They had become the only family she'd ever really known.

She had also been in desperate need of a job, and her father, a man she'd only seen a handful of times in her life, had introduced her to a family in need of a nanny while the children were out of school for the summer holiday. She'd performed the job so well that the family had kept her on for the coming school year. She helped with the children, and their schoolwork, and ferrying them from one after-school activity to another. She'd stayed with that family until the parents divorced and could no longer keep her on, but she'd found another job right away, and then another until she'd realized that she couldn't continue in child care—all the goodbyes were too hard on her heart—and she went to work in retail.

She'd started downstairs at the register in hats and gloves, and then when they were short-staffed in bridal, went to the fifth floor to fill in, and had never left the bridal department. If others thought she was too young to be the manager of the department at twenty-six, no one said so, because despite her age, she had style and flair and an eye for quality. Monet wasn't entirely surprised. She was her mother's daughter after all.

"I know this is a lot to take in so I propose we postpone further conversation until you've finished here, and we can go to dinner and relax and have a civilized discussion." Marcu gave her an encouraging smile. "It will give you an opportunity to ask the questions that I'm sure will come to you—"

"But I have no questions," she interrupted, refusing to fall for his charm, painfully aware that in the past she'd found Marcu nearly irresistible—and he knew it, too. He knew exactly how to play her, just as he'd successfully played her eight years ago. She had no wish to fall in with his plans again and rose, indicating she was finished with the conversation.

"Marcu, I have no interest in this position. It's pointless to continue as I have no wish to waste your time, nor do I wish to waste my own. I'm to return here early tomorrow morning and I still need to find a missing gown before Mrs. Wilkerson descends on us again." She drew another short, tight breath. "I wish I could say it was good to see you, but that would be a lie, and after all these years there is no point in either of us lying to the other."

"I never imagined you to be vindictive."

"Vindictive? Not at all. Just because I can't fall in line with your plans doesn't mean I harbor you ill will. You were important to me once. But that was years and years ago."

He rose as well, and he towered over her now. "You made me a promise, Monet. I'm afraid you can't say no…at least not yet, not until you have heard me out, and you haven't. You don't know the details. You don't know the time frame. You don't know the salary, or the benefits."

She threw up her hands. "There are no benefits to working for you!"

"You once loved us. You used to say that we were the family you never had."

"I was young and naive. I know better now."

"Did something happen after you left Palermo? Did something occur that I do not know about?"

"No. You know everything."

"Then why so much scorn and hatred for my family? How did they hurt you?"

She couldn't immediately answer, not when her emotions bubbled up, her chest too hot and tender. She had once loved them all. She had once dreamed of being part of them, a cherished member of the family. But that wasn't to be. She wasn't one of them. She hadn't any hope of being one of them. Her eyes stung, and her throat ached. Monet fought to speak. "It was good of your family to tolerate me for so many years, especially in light of who I was. So no, I do not hate your entire family. I do not speak of your brother and sisters with scorn."

"So your anger is with me, and my father, then?"

This is precisely what she didn't want to do. Dredge up the past. Relive the old pain. She dug her nails into her palms, fighting for control. "It doesn't matter. I don't wish to discuss it. I don't live in the past, and neither should you."

"Unfortunately, it does matter to me, and unfortunately you are in my debt, so we will discuss it later, over dinner. I shall leave you now to finish up here. My car will be downstairs waiting for you. I look forward to continuing our discussion then." He nodded at her and walked away, heading for the gleaming elevators against the distant wall.

She stood there watching him until the elevators opened and he stepped in. He never once turned around until he was inside the elevator and then, and only then, did he turn and look back to find her still standing where he'd left her. Their gazes met and held, a fierce silent challenge that was only broken by the closing of the doors.

He crossed his arms over his chest and exhaled in the privacy of the elevator. Marcu hadn't missed the challenge in Monet's eyes, or her defiant expression as she'd stared him down until the elevator doors closed, blocking the view. He'd expected some resistance from her but this was ridiculous. Monet Wilde needed to remember that she owed him, and not the other way around.

Further, she hadn't been his first pick for child care.

He hadn't even thought of her until after he'd exhausted every resource, trying to find someone already familiar with his children to take care of them over the Christmas holidays. Their nanny of the past two and a half years had a family emergency and needed to be with her own parents, and he understood that it was an emergency but Marcu was now in a terrible bind because he wouldn't let just anyone be with his children. He was very selective, very protective, and he needed more than a warm body to mind his three young children over Christmas. Marcu hadn't even thought of Monet until the last woman he'd interviewed for the position had exited the room and he'd faced the window, disappointed, and deeply troubled. He didn't want his children to be with a stranger.

He didn't trust strangers.

But then, he didn't trust many people, period.

He was well aware that his lack of trust was a problem. It had been a problem for much of his adult life, resulting in a tendency to overanalyze, which wasn't a bad thing as a venture capitalist, but an issue when it came to his social life. Until very recently he'd refused to extend himself beyond his small, trusted inner circle, but when it became obvious that his inner circle would not provide him with a replacement wife to mother his young children, he'd been forced to go further afield. After a series of excruciating dates he'd found a suitable prospect in twenty-nine-year-old Vittoria Bonfiglio, and it was his plan to propose to her on Christmas

Eve, but first, he needed some time alone with her, something difficult to achieve when his children were running wild while their nanny was at home in England with her family.

Which is when Monet came to mind. He hadn't thought of her in years, and yet once he'd thought of her, she seemed to be the perfect solution.

He knew her, and she'd never once betrayed his trust. She'd always been good with his younger brother and sisters—why wouldn't she be as patient and kind with his three?

And once Marcu set his mind on something, it was relatively easy to make things happen. It took him less than fifteen minutes to locate her—she lived in London, and worked at Bernard Department Store. She wasn't married. She might have a boyfriend. Marcu didn't care. He needed her for four weeks, five weeks tops, and then she could return to her life in retail and he'd have his new bride and his child-care issue would be permanently sorted.

It didn't cross his mind that she'd say no, because she owed him. She'd left Palermo in his debt and he was calling in the favor.

* * *

Even after Marcu was gone, Monet couldn't move. She was too stunned to do anything but wish the ground would swallow her whole.

All she'd wanted today was to go home after work, take a long hot bath, change into cozy pajamas and curl up on her couch and stream her favorite television programs, lost in the pleasure of diverting entertainment.

She wouldn't be going home anytime soon now.

There would be no long hot bath or a satisfying hour or two of her favorite program.

Slowly she turned, her gaze sweeping the fifth floor. Over the years this elegant, luxurious space had come to feel more like home than her own flat. She was good at what she did. She knew how to soothe the nervous bride, and organize the overwhelmed one. Who would have thought this would be her gift, never mind her skill set?

The illegitimate daughter of a struggling French actress and an English banker, Monet had a most unusual and Bohemian upbringings. By eighteen, she had seen far more of the world than her peers, having lived in Ireland, France,

Sicily, Morocco, and three different American states.

She'd spent the longest stretch in Sicily, Palermo being her home for six years from the time she was nearly twelve until she'd turned eighteen. Even after she'd left Palermo, her mother had continued to live with Sicilian aristocrat Matteo Uberto for another three years. But after leaving, Monet never returned to Sicily. She didn't want to see any of the Uberto family, and she'd rebuffed Marcu when he tried to visit her in London three years ago, just as she'd rebuffed his father a year earlier when Matteo appeared on her doorstep with wine and flowers and a delicate negligee more appropriate for your paramour than your former lover's daughter. It was that visit by Matteo that ensured she finally closed the door on the past, locking it securely.

She had nothing in common with this family she had lived with for six years of her life. Yes, they'd shared meals together, and yes, they'd gone to the movies, and various plays, ballets, and operas together, as well as shared holidays at the beach and Christmases at the palazzo, but in the end she was not one of them, not a member of the family, or a member of Sicilian aristocratic society.

No, she was the bastard daughter of a careless British banker, and a French actress more famous for her affairs and her wealthy lovers then her acting talent, and therefore to be treated as someone cheap and unimportant.

Monet could live with cheap. She couldn't bear to be unimportant, though. She didn't need to be valued by the world, but she'd craved Marcu's love, and respect.

Instead he'd been the first to shame her, but Monet was a quick learner, and she vowed to never be dependent on anyone again, and she hadn't been.

Determined to be different from her mother in every way, she not only rejected all things scandalous, but also pushed away her colorful, Bohemian past. She was no longer Candie's daughter. She was no longer vulnerable, or apologetic. She was herself, her own creation and invention. Unlike her mother, Monet didn't need men. It might not be fair, but it was easier to view them with suspicion than be open to their advances.

It didn't stop men from pursuing her, though,

and they did. They were intrigued by her very French cheekbones, pouting lips, golden-brown eyes and long thick dark hair, but they didn't know her, and they didn't realize that while she might look like a siren on the outside, she was British on the inside, and not about to indulge in meaningless affairs. She wasn't interested in sex, which is why at twenty-six, she was still a virgin, and quite possibly frigid. Monet didn't care if she was. She wasn't interested in labels, nor did she care what men thought, aware that to most men, women were just toys—playthings—and she had no desire to be anyone's plaything. Her mother, Matteo, and Marcu Uberto had made sure of that.

CHAPTER TWO

AN HOUR LATER Monet was outside, and the black car was where Marcu said it would be, parked in front of Bernard's front doors. The driver appeared the moment she stepped outside, and he opened a large black umbrella to protect her from the flurries of snow. She murmured her thanks as she stepped into the car.

She glimpsed Marcu and held her breath, careful to keep a distance between them.

"So what exactly do you do here?" he asked, as the car pulled away from the curb, sliding into the stream of traffic.

She placed her purse on her lap, and rested her hands on the purse clasp. "Manage the department. Assist brides finding their dream gown. Keep mothers from overwhelming their emotional daughters."

"An interesting choice for you, given your background."

Her chin notched up. "Because my mother

never married?" she asked, a dark elegant winged eyebrow arching higher.

Of course he'd find it ironic that she'd work as a bridal-gown consultant, but most people didn't know her background. In fact, the only ones who knew her background were the father who'd never been part of her life and the Uberto family.

"Any problems closing?" he asked a moment later, his tone one of excessive politeness.

She nearly rolled her eyes. Surely they were beyond such superficial pleasantries. "No."

"Were you working at Bernard's when I reached out to you a few years ago?"

"I was. I've been there for four years now."

"Why wouldn't you see me when I reached out to you?" he asked.

Her shoulders lifted, and fell. "There was no point." She turned her head, her gaze resting on his hard masculine profile illuminated by the streetlights. He had a perfect face—broad brow, straight, strong nose, wide firm lips, angled jaw, square chin. And yet it wasn't the individual features that made him attractive, it was the way they came together—the quirk of his lips, the creases at the corner of his eyes, the blue gleam in his eyes. She steeled herself against the curve of his lips and the piercing blue of his eyes now. "Was there?"

"I don't understand," he answered simply.

"You were a married man. I was a single woman. I didn't see what good could come of us meeting."

"I wasn't coming to you for sex."

"How was I to know? Your father did."

"What?"

She shrugged again, exhausted by the day, and his appearance. Her exhaustion made her careless. Why keep all these secrets? Why not tell the truth? "Your father approached me a year before you did. He came bearing gifts."

"Your mother had just passed away. He was just being kind."

"Then perhaps a casserole would have been proper. But roses? A pink satin robe? It was wildly inappropriate."

"He gave my sisters a similar robe each for Christmas one year—pink, even. Why must you make his gift sound scandalous?"

Because he didn't like me, Monet thought, turning her head to stare out the window, regretting her words. Why share such a thing with Marcu? Of course he wouldn't believe her. He'd always worshipped his father. Matteo Uberto could do no wrong.

Silence stretched. They sat forever at the next stop light. The snow was heavier, wetter, and it stuck to the glass in thick clumps.

"I wasn't interested in making you my mistress," Marcu said roughly, breaking the tense silence. "I came to see you as my wife had just died and I needed advice. I thought you could help me. I was wrong."

His words created a lance of pain. Her stomach knotted and her chest grew tight. "I'm sorry. I didn't know."

"But you did know I'd married?"

She nodded. He'd married just six months after she left Palermo. She hadn't wanted to know but it was splashed across the tabloids as well as the internet as the Uberto family was wealthy, glamorous, aristocratic, and very much darlings of the media.

Marcu's wedding was held at the cathedral in Palermo, a place she knew well as that was where the Uberto family attended church services every Sunday. Marcu had married an Italian countess from northern Italy, although her maternal grandmother was Sicilian. Galeta Corrado was an only child and stood to inherit all the ancestral homes and estates of her family, a family that could be traced back hundreds of years. Marcu's family was considerably older, his ancestors Sicilian royalty dating back five hundred years, a fact the tabloids mentioned ad nauseam in their coverage of the Uberto-Corrado wedding, sharing that Marcu's great-grandfather had been a Sicilian prince, and Marcu could probably claim the title, but he was far too egalitarian.

He wasn't.

Monet could scarcely stomach that one.

Marcu and Galeta's wedding had been lavish, with Galeta's bridal gown costing close to forty thousand euros. The silk train stretched for yards, with the hand-crocheted lace veil equally long, the delicate lace anchored to a priceless two-hundred-year-old pink diamond-and-pearl tiara. The bride had been a stunning vision in white, her slender form showcased by the luminous silk. The first baby came not quite nine months later. There was gossip that Galeta was pregnant at the time she married, and it was then Monet had refused to read the tabloids ever again. She was done. Spent. Flattened.

She didn't want to know anything else. She didn't want to live on the fringes of Marcu's life. She didn't want to know about his wife or children. She refused to look back, refused to remember, unwilling to feel the pain that washed through her every time his name was mentioned.

The pain baffled her, too, because when she left Palermo, she'd convinced herself that she hadn't loved him, she'd merely been infatuated. She'd told herself she felt curiosity and desire, but not true love. So why did his name hurt? Why did his marriage wound? It wasn't until he'd married Galeta and they'd had that first baby together, that Monet realized her feelings for him were stronger and deeper than she'd previously allowed herself to acknowledge. She couldn't possibly hurt so much if she'd merely been infatuated. She wouldn't miss him so much if she'd just been curious. No, she hurt because she loved him, and he was only the second person in her whole life she'd ever loved.

Monet turned back to Marcu again, still not

quite able to believe he was here, beside her. She felt so many different things, and her chaotic emotions weren't improved by his close proximity. Marcu had been handsome at twenty, and twenty-five, but now, at thirty-three, his face was even more arresting. He'd matured, the bones in his jaw and cheekbones more defined, the hollows beneath his cheekbones more pronounced, his skin lightly tanned, glowing with health and vitality.

"How did she die?" Monet asked, trying to organize her thoughts, never mind her impossible emotions.

"She had a stroke after childbirth." He drew a breath. "I'd never heard of such a thing but our doctor said that while it's uncommon, strokes cause ten percent of all pregnancy-related deaths." He was silent another moment. "I wasn't even there when it happened. I'd just flown to New York, thinking she was in good hands at the palazzo with the nanny and night nurse."

"You don't blame yourself, do you?"

"I don't blame myself for the stroke, but I can't forget that she died while I was on a plane over the Atlantic Ocean. It wasn't right. It shouldn't have been that way. If I'd been there, maybe I could have gotten her help sooner. Maybe the doctors could have saved her."

Monet didn't know how to respond and so she sat there with the distressing words resonating around her, listening to the soft rhythmic sweep of the windshield wipers moving back and forth, clearing the glass, even as her heart did a painful beat in her chest.

Of course Marcu would feel badly. How could he not feel partially responsible? But at the same time, that didn't make his situation her problem. He needed help, yes, but why from her?

"Does your late wife have no family who could help with the children?" she asked as the traffic thinned. They were approaching London's commercial financial hub, and during the week the streets bustled with activity but now the area was quiet and dark. "What of Galeta's parents? No grandparents to lend a supportive hand?"

"Galeta was an only child, and her parents are both gone. My father is gone. I have my brother and sisters, but they all are busy with their own lives."

"Just as I am busy with my own life," she retorted lightly, unwilling to escalate things in the close confines of his car.

"I'm asking for a few weeks, not years."

She glanced out the window and watched the grand Bank of England pass by. Lovingly referred to as the Old Lady of Threadneedle Street by some, Monet was always awed and reassured by its history and size. "It's simply not a good time," she answered, glancing from the bank to Marcu.

"Would any time be a good time?" he countered.

The car turned at the corner, passing more historic buildings that formed the heart of the city of London, making Monet wonder where they were going to eat in this particular neighborhood before her attention returned to Marcu.

"No," she answered with a sigh, even as she reached up to tuck a long tendril behind her ear. She was tired and uncomfortable and she wanted out of her slim dress and heels. She wanted the delicate underwire bra off and the smoothing undergarments off so that she could climb into pajamas and eat warm comfort food and sip a big glass of red wine. Merlot. Burgundy. Shiraz. "I have no desire to work for you, ever."

"I know," he answered even as the driver pulled over in front of one of the big dark buildings, parked, and exited the driver's side, again wielding the umbrella. He opened the back door and Marcu stepped out and then reached in to assist her. She avoided his hand, neatly stepping away to make sure there was no contact between them.

He shot her a sardonic glance but said nothing as the driver walked them to a plain wooden door. Marcu reached out and touched one gray stone. There was a long pause and then the door silently opened. They stepped inside a dimly lit, severe-looking entrance hall. The door closed behind them and Monet gazed around, curious but also confused by the stillness and emptiness of the impersonal cream-and-gray space. There were stairs at the back of the hallway and a service elevator to their right but that was all.

"I normally prefer the stairs," Marcu said, "but you've been on your feet all day, so I suggest we take the elevator."

They did, traveling down, but it was impossible to say how far down they went, before the doors silently opened, revealing a black-and-white marble parquet floor, massive columns, and what looked like the entrance to a huge bank vault. Walls glimmered gold and silver on the other side of the vault entrance. She glanced at Marcu, an eyebrow lifting in silent enquiry.

He gestured for her to proceed through the open vault door, where they were greeted by a gentleman in a dark suit and black shirt. "Mr. Uberto," the man said. "It's good to have you back."

They were ushered past an elegant bar of stainless steel and thick glass where a bartender was mixing drinks, then through another archway to a dining room dotted with chandeliers. The chandeliers were an eclectic mix of styles and time periods, and hung from a silver ceiling casting soft pools of light on pale lavender velvet chairs and upholstered booths. There weren't more than a dozen tables in the room. There were men at some tables, and couples at others. Monet and Marcu were taken to yet another room, this one small and private, with just one table. The chandelier was all pink glass, and the upholstery on the high back chairs was gray.

Monet sank into her well-upholstered chair with an appreciative sigh. It felt even more welcoming than it looked. "This is quite a place," she said, as waiters appeared in quick succession with bottles of chilled mineral water, olives, and pâté with slivers of toasted baguette.

"It was once part of the Bank of Sicily. It's now a private members' club."

"I suspected as much." She reached for an olive and popped it in her mouth, suddenly ravenous. "Let me guess, your father used to have a membership here, and they extended an invitation to you?"

"My grandfather used to own the bank, my father closed it, and when he couldn't find someone to buy the building for its proper value, I took it on and turned the Vault into a private club five years ago."

"What happened to the rest of the building?"

"It's now a members-only hotel and spa."

"Do you use the same door to access the hotel and spa?"

"No, there is a different entrance."

"Why?"

"Because membership to the hotel doesn't give one automatic membership to the Vault."

"Is this where you stay when you're in London?"

"The top floor is my apartment, yes."

"It's quite spacious."

"You don't make that sound like a question," he replied, leaning back in his chair.

"It's not," she answered, before thanking the waiter who presented her with a silver menu. She glanced down at it, scanning the delectable offerings. She could have been perfectly happy with just pâté and toast but once she spotted the flat-iron steak she knew what she wanted.

After ordering, Marcu got straight to the point. "I do need you, urgently. I would have liked to leave tonight, but obviously it's too late now. So I'll organize travel for the morning—"

"Marcu, I haven't said yes."

"But you will."

She rolled her eyes, frustrated, and yet part of her frustration was based on the truth in his words. She did owe him. "January would be so much better for me."

"I've already told you, I have a conference in the Far East in January, and I would like to have things sorted by then."

"Sorted as in…?"

"Married, with Vittoria at home with the children. I worry more about the children when I am far away. This way they'd have their nanny, Miss Sheldon, who's on leave at the moment, and a mother—"

"But they don't have a close relationship with this new mother, do they?"

"They've been introduced."

She felt a bubble of incredulous laughter. "I don't know who to feel more sorry for, your future wife, or your children. Where is your sensitivity—?"

"Oh, that's long gone. I'm as hard as they come now."

"Your poor future wife."

"I'm not romantic. I never have been."

"So says the man who loved opera? Who'd listen to Puccini for hours?"

"*You* loved opera. I simply supported your passion."

She eyed him, trying to come to terms with this new version of Marcu. He was so hard to stomach. "You do know you'd be better off hiring a new nanny, or even two, to job-share than trying to fix things by acquiring a wife. Wives do come with feelings—"

"Not all women require extravagant gestures. Vittoria is quite practical. And I'm hoping you can be practical, too. I'll pay you one hundred thousand euros for the next five weeks," he added. "Hopefully that will adequately cover any lost wages from Bernard's."

"And if they don't take me back afterward?"

"You will continue to earn twenty thousand euros a week until I find you a new position."

She was intrigued and appalled. "That's a lot of money."

"My children are worth it."

"So you are still consumed with guilt over your wife's death."

"I'm not consumed with guilt, just determined to make amends. They are very good children, but they are also in need of a mother. I do not, and cannot, meet all their needs, which is why I'm determined to marry again. A mother will be better equipped to handle their ups and downs and various emotions."

"This mother you speak of will be practically a stranger to them."

"But they will form a relationship. I don't expect it to happen overnight, but I do believe it will happen eventually, and I imagine when a new baby arrives, the children will be excited to have a new brother or sister."

Monet studied him for a long moment. Did he really think his children, who had already been deprived of a mother, would welcome the competition of a new baby for their father's attention? "I remember you studied finance at university. It's a shame you didn't study more psychology. Creating a new family isn't an easy thing, and children who have been through loss and heartbreak don't always welcome more change."

"I don't expect them to understand immediately. They are still very young but their innocence is also to their advantage. They will be grateful for a permanent mother figure. As it is they are very attached to their current nanny, and I fear the day Miss Sheldon leaves us for good."

"I thought your nanny was only on temporary leave?"

"So she is, but I see the writing on the wall. It's only a matter of time." He hesitated. "Miss Sheldon has fallen in love with my pilot. They've been secretly dating for the past year.

They don't think I know, but neither of them are as discreet as they imagine."

"Your nanny couldn't marry and continue working for you?"

"They will want to start a family of their own. She's in her thirties. I know how these things go. She's not our first nanny, nor will she be the last."

"But she hasn't left yet—"

"I don't care to discuss Miss Sheldon with you. I'm simply informing you that you will not lose any wages while you work for me."

His brusque tone put her teeth on edge. His arrogance was beyond off-putting. The very idea of working for him made her nauseous. She'd had so many feelings for him, but none of them involved being his employee. She didn't want him as her superior. The idea of having to answer to him made her want to stand up and storm out. She'd thought she'd loved him once—desperately, passionately—but he'd deemed her unsuitable. Unworthy.

Suddenly she flashed back to another conversation, one between Marcu and his father as they'd discussed how inappropriate Monet was for someone of Marcu's stature. That Monet might be sweet and charming but she was the kind of woman you took as your mistress, not as your wife.

To hear this at eighteen. To be so painfully and thoroughly dismissed, reduced—*marginalized*—at only eighteen. It had changed her forever.

"I can't work for you," she said in a low voice. "I can't be at your beck and call."

"I won't be around after the first few days. I'll only be there to get you settled and then I'm taking Vittoria to Altapura for Christmas. She loves to ski. She's a very good skier, too, so unless something unexpected happens, we'll return just after New Year."

"You won't be spending the holidays with your children?" she asked, confused.

"No. That's the whole point of me seeking you out. I won't be with them this year, but you will be."

Monet felt another welling of pity for his children. It was also difficult to believe that Marcu had become such a cold, pragmatic man. He'd been so warm and kind when he was younger. He'd been a very loving, and much-adored, big brother. "Do they know this?"

"They know that it's going to be a different kind of holiday this year. I haven't told them more than that. I didn't think it appropriate until Vittoria accepts my proposal."

"You worry me, Marcu, and you make me worry for the children, too."

Marcu's eyes met hers and held, the light blue gaze heavily hooded, and assessing. "They are not mistreated in any way."

"They'll miss you."

"They won't. They might even be relieved to have me gone." He hesitated. "I know they have more fun with Miss Sheldon when I'm away."

"And that doesn't bother you?"

"I never asked to be both mother and father."

"But leaving them altogether seems exceptionally unfair—"

"It seems you want to fight with me. Does it give you pleasure? I've already told you I'm not good at this parenting thing. I have not been a rousing success. What more do you want from me?"

The raw pain in his voice silenced her. She sat still for a moment, feeling his deep anguish echo in her ears. She waited another moment until she was sure she could speak calmly. "I don't want to fight with you, but I'm not comfortable with the way things ended between us. And while I'm sympathetic to your children's situation—they've experienced loss and grief and they need stability—I also recognize that I'm not the right person to fill in for your nanny."

"Why not? You're very good with children."

"I only did child care temporarily, until I found permanent work. Further, I can't leave Bernard's on such short notice. I was down two saleswomen in my department today. It's impossible for my department to run without anybody there tomorrow. I must speak with management. I must clear things—"

"I already have," he interrupted flatly. "I had a brief conversation this morning with Charles."

"Bernard?"

Marcu's dark head inclined impatiently. "He was sorry to hear of my emergency, and agreed that you would be the best help for me—"

"Emergency? What emergency?" She exhaled hard, battling to keep her temper in check. "You've decided to go skiing with your girlfriend during the same time period your nanny needs a break. That's not an emergency."

"I have no dedicated help for them."

"Then do what others in your situation do—hire a replacement through a professional service. You refuse to, but that doesn't constitute an emergency."

He shrugged. "You're wrong. Charles agreed that young children cannot be left with a stranger. Once he understood your connection with my family, he thought you were the best answer."

Such a power play. What arrogance! Monet was shocked at how manipulative Marcu had been. "I can't believe you went to my boss and told him some ridiculous sob story. I'm sorry that your nanny needed a break just now, and I'm sorry you had plans to ski—"

"It's not about the skiing. I'm going to propose—"

"Regardless, that's not my problem, and I'm livid that you've spoken to anyone about me, much less the CEO of Bernard's."

"I didn't think it'd hurt you in any way for Charles to know that we have a close family connection. If anything, it will help your standing on your return. I'm quite certain you will see more promotions, and more salary increases."

"Did you happen to tell Charles just what our close family connection was? Did you explain to him that my mother was your father's mistress? Charles is quite conservative—"

"He knows our connection, just as he knows you are Edward Wilde's daughter. Your father is on the board at Bernard's. I suspect your rapid promotions have had something to do with that."

Her mouth opened, closed. She had no idea that her father was on the board. She hadn't spoken to him in years...not since he'd provided references, helping her get her first nanny job. "I earned my promotions through hard work, not through family connections."

"Your father is quite respected in the banking world."

"That has nothing to do with me. I've seen him less than a half dozen times in my life. He had no interest in me, and only gave me those references I needed because I went to him, and told him I needed his assistance. He balked, at first, but came around when I threatened to introduce myself to his wife and children."

Marcu lifted a black brow. "You don't think they already knew about you?"

"I'm sure they didn't, and that's fine. Everyone makes mistakes and my mother was Edward's mistake."

"You call him Edward?"

"I certainly don't call him Father."

"You're more defensive than ever."

"I'm not defensive. He didn't want me, and he paid my mother to get rid of me. Instead she took the money and went to the States and then Morocco and you know the rest. Edward tolerates my existence because he has no other choice. Just as your father tolerated me because he had no other choice. As a young girl I had to accept that I was barely tolerated, but I don't anymore." She drew a quick breath. "This is why I can't do this favor for you. I won't be treated as a second-class citizen any longer. It's not acceptable. Not from you, not from anyone."

"I never treated you as a second-class citizen."

"You did at the end, you know you did."

"What are you talking about? Does this have something to do with the kiss?"

Heat flashed through her, making her shake. "It was more than a kiss."

"You welcomed my attention. Don't pretend you didn't."

"You did not force yourself on me, no. But what I thought was happening was quite different from reality."

"I don't understand."

She drew a breath and then another, battling to hang on to the last thread of her composure. Crying would be a disaster. Losing control would be the final humiliation. She refused to endure any more shame. "We were not equals. You let me imagine we were. But we weren't."

"I still don't understand."

"It doesn't matter. It's no longer relevant. But what is relevant is my answer today. It's a no. If I had wanted to be part of your life I would have stayed in Palermo, but I left for a reason and I have no desire to spend time with you. Ever. Which is why I'm demanding you forgive the debt, forget the favor, and let me let leave now with us both closing the door on the past, once and forever."

Marcu froze, her words catching him off guard because yes, they probably both needed to close the door on the past and yet, it was the last thing he wanted.

And in that moment he realized something else.

Marcu hadn't been honest when he told himself Monet wasn't his first choice for a backup nanny. That was a lie. He'd interviewed plenty of candidates, but none of them had been right for the job, because none of them had been Monet. He'd been dismissive of the other women, finding fault with each, precisely so he could come to Monet today and say, *I need you*.

Because he did.

He needed her to come help him stabilize things at home while he figured out how to give his children a better life.

His children needed more than him. He wasn't patient and tender, or particularly affectionate. He loved his children but he didn't know how to meet all their needs, which is why he needed a partner...a better half. He needed a wife, someone maternal, someone to create stability in their home. He traveled too much. He worked too long. He was constantly at war with himself, juggling his business commitments while trying to be present with the children—not easy when his main office was in New York and his children were being raised in Sicily. He'd fly to New York for three days, but inevitably he'd have to extend his trip by a day, and then another, and another. Sometimes his brief trips became a week long and then two weeks, and he not only worried about the kids, but he'd also be filled with guilt and self-loathing.

Guilt that Galeta had died.

Self-loathing because he didn't want to remarry and it's why he hadn't proposed to someone sooner.

Galeta had been a kind, loyal wife, and while they didn't have a passionate marriage, they became friends and partners, with Galeta creating a warm loving home for him and their children in the main apartment at the palazzo. Her death had been a shock, and it had taken him years to wrap his head around the tragedy. Why hadn't he known that a woman was still so vulnerable after delivery? Why had he thought that once she was home from the hospital everything was fine?

The guilt. The agony. She had deserved better, and so did their children. He wasn't the father he'd thought he would be. He wasn't good enough at all. And so while he didn't want another wife, he would remarry, and he'd make sure that his new wife understood that her first responsibility was to the children.

"I can't forgive the favor because I need you," he replied now, his rough tone betraying his impatience. "You needed help from me eight years ago, and I helped you, and now I'm asking for you to return the favor. You understand this, I know you do. You lived with us long enough to understand our Sicilian view of these things."

Monet gave her dark head a faint shake. Two bright spots of color stained her cheekbones, while her large golden-brown eyes glowed, burning with emotion.

"I also know that you could choose to be magnanimous and forgive the debt."

"If my children weren't involved, then yes, perhaps I could. But this is about my children, and they need you, which is why I need you."

She slowly sat back in her chair, her slim frame practically vibrating with fury. She was both beautiful and fierce, and it struck him that he'd never seen this side of her before.

In Palermo she'd been quiet and sweet with a deliciously dry sense of humor. She rarely spoke when his father was present, but when she was with Marcu and his brother and sisters, she had plenty to say, and inevitably she made everyone laugh. He should have known that underneath her sweet persona she had backbone. He was pleased to see it, finding it something of a relief. His world was filled with people who acquiesced to his every desire simply because he was wealthy and powerful. But it was hard to trust people who claimed they always agreed with you and only wanted to please you. Those people were dangerous. They could be bought.

"I don't like you," she said quietly, carefully, the lushness of her lower lip quivering before she pressed her mouth into a firm line.

Her words hung there between them, coloring the private dining room. He let them hover, too, even though his first instinct was to remind her that once she'd followed him everywhere, had been absolutely devoted to him, and was always the first to defend him even though he'd never needed her defense. No, he'd never needed it but her loyalty had always touched him, and in return he'd kept an eye out for her, been protective of her even when he'd been away at university. He'd paid one of the palazzo staff to report to him because he worried about her in his absence. Her mother was oblivious to her existence and while his father would never hurt her, he only tolerated the girl for Candie's sake.

It was never good to merely be tolerated. Monet was too smart, too sensitive not to have been aware of her position in the Uberto household.

"Now," he said, breaking the silence. "You don't like me *now*. We both know that wasn't always the case."

"But that dislike should be enough for you to not want me to be with your children. That dislike should make you reject me as a suitable caregiver."

"Your dislike is at least honest. I respect such honesty, and I also know that you are far too fair to allow your personal feelings for me to prejudice you against my children."

"But you don't know me. I'm not the girl who

left Palermo eight years ago with nothing but a knapsack on her back—"

"And five thousand of my euros in your pocket."

"Don't you understand?" she blurted, rising swiftly to her feet. "I didn't want your money then, and I don't want it now."

She would have fled if he'd allowed it. He wasn't going to let her go, though. His hand snaked out and wrapped around her wrist, preventing her from leaving.

"Sit down," he said quietly. "Have a conversation with me."

"There is no point," she said hotly. "You don't listen. You're not hearing what I'm saying." She tugged to free herself. He didn't let go. "Why can't you offer a compromise? Why can't you meet me partway? I can't leave my job now. I would be willing to do it in January—"

"I don't need you in January," he interrupted, releasing her, hoping she would sit. She didn't. She continued to stand there at the table, furious and indignant. "Miss Sheldon will be back then," he added. "Once she's back, I won't need you."

"I can't leave my work for up to five weeks.

It's mid-December now. That means I'd still be gone in the middle of January."

"Four weeks then." He suppressed a sigh. "Will you sit, please?"

"That's still the middle of January."

He was silent a long moment before countering. "Three weeks from tomorrow, but only if you sit down. This is uncomfortable, and we're drawing attention."

"There is no one else in this dining room. It's exceptionally private."

"I'm in this dining room and you're making me uncomfortable."

"Heavens, we can't have that, can we?" she retorted mockingly, before slowly sitting back down. "Two weeks."

"Three."

She reached for her wineglass and took a sip, hoping he wouldn't see how her hand trembled. "I wouldn't want to remain after you and Vittoria return after New Year's."

"You wouldn't have to."

"I'll be on a flight home that first weekend of January."

"I'll send you home on my plane. I promise."

Her gaze met his. "Or sooner if you and Vittoria return sooner. I've no interest in being present while you integrate Vittoria into your household."

"Understood."

"And one more stipulation," she said after a long pause. "I need to go to work in the morning. I must find a missing wedding gown—"

"We need to return to Italy."

"*You* need to return to Italy. I don't." Her eyebrows lifted as her brown eyes flashed indignant fire. "*I* need to find Mrs. Wilkerson's daughter's missing gown, and then I can go with you. Give me until noon. I've made Mrs. Wilkerson a promise and a promise is a promise."

He digested her words for a moment before brusquely nodding. "Fine. My car will be at Bernard's at noon. We will leave straight for the airport."

The corner of her mouth curled up. "You're not worried that I'll try to run away and escape you?"

His body went hard at that saucy curl of her lips. Thank God he wasn't going to be spending much time with Monet. Thank God he was taking her to the *castello* and leaving promptly.

Monet had always tested his control. She still tested his control.

"No," he answered roughly. "Because a promise is a promise."

CHAPTER THREE

MONET KEPT HER eyes closed during the flight over the jagged peaks of southeastern France lit by the setting sun. She wasn't afraid of flying, but this afternoon her stomach thumped, queasy with anxiety and dread.

She couldn't quite believe this was happening.

Christmas in the Italian Alps. Christmas with Marcu—correction, Christmas with Marcu's children, as Marcu would be elsewhere, wooing his future wife.

As a girl she'd dreaded the Christmas holidays. There had been years where she and her mother didn't celebrate Christmas at all, and then there were years where they celebrated someone else's holiday traditions, and when she was little Monet had found it confusing. So many people seemed to love Christmas but for her it was often incredibly painful.

She didn't really experience a proper Christmas until she and her mother moved to Palermo. Her best Christmas memories had been with the Uberto family at their palazzo. The Ubertos celebrated Christmas in a grand way, their December filled with music and food, gifts and sweets. But even in Palermo, Christmas had been about the Uberto children and their father and their aristocratic Sicilian heritage. Monet had merely been that odd French-English girl who kept to the background to avoid drawing unnecessary attention to herself. It was better for her, and better for her mother, who didn't really want to be a mother but loved Monet just enough to keep her daughter with her, but not enough to do what was right for her.

Uneasy with the memories, Monet stirred and opened her eyes to glance out the window. As she looked up her gaze briefly met Marcu's. He was still at his table, working on some pile of paperwork. Obviously he wasn't so engrossed in his work that he was oblivious to her, and Monet wasn't sure how that made her feel.

"This is a terrible idea," she said huskily. "We will both regret this."

"I won't regret it. I need help, and I know my children will be in good hands with you."

Monet regarded him from beneath her lashes. He was so arrogant and self-assured. As well as shockingly handsome. He had been incredibly good-looking as a young adult, but now as a mature man, his face was all strong angles and planes, slashing cheekbones, broad, strong brow, firm mouth, firmer chin. His thick black hair was swept back from his face, framing piercing blue eyes, and a counterbalance to straight white teeth. His face alone would turn heads, but paired with his tall, lithe, muscular frame, he was beautiful indeed.

It would be easier, sitting here, if she didn't find him physically appealing. It would be easier if her heart didn't jump every time he glanced her way.

She'd forgotten that she could even feel this kind of fear and anxiety flooding her. It was the fear she'd felt as a girl, the fear that made it hard to breathe properly and therefore her head would spin, feeling light and dizzy.

She felt dizzy now.

She felt angry, too, that he'd forced her into this job. She wasn't a nanny anymore. She had a career. She had responsibility and work she enjoyed and yet he'd insisted she drop everything for this stupid "favor."

She closed her hands, fingers curling into her palms, nails digging in sharply to try to contain her crippling anxiety. The tension was almost unbearable. This was such a terrible mistake and there was nothing she could do it about it.

"Did you find your customer's missing wedding gown?" Marcu asked suddenly, his voice surprisingly close.

She opened her eyes and shuddered to see that he'd left his desk and was seated opposite her now in the pale cream leather chair that matched hers. He was by no means sprawled in his seat and yet his long legs seemed to fill up the space, and his imposing shoulders drew her attention up to his face, and those cool blue watchful eyes. He felt far too relaxed for her peace of mind. She hadn't heard him approach or sit down. She should have. Her skin prickled with unease. She wasn't afraid of him, but rather, was afraid of all he made her feel—the anger, the shame, the heartbreak. "I did, yes," she answered. "It was in alterations, but had been mislabeled. Crisis averted."

"Your customer must have been very relieved."

"Not as much as I was. It was a very expensive gown."

Marcu lowered his blind partway, blocking the glare from the setting sun. "I'm still trying to come to terms with you as a bridal consultant."

"Is it really so shocking?" she asked, aware it had never been her goal or dream to work with brides, but it turned out she had a knack for finding the right dress for the right woman who wanted nothing less than spectacular for her wedding day. It seemed that Monet had somehow absorbed her actress mother's knack for the theatrical, and coupled with her own artistic flair, as well as with the hefty measure of patience required when working with emotional, temperamental brides, Monet had worked her way up from fetching gowns from the back room to managing Bernard's entire department.

"There is a great deal of theater in a wedding," she added thoughtfully. "My mother was an actress. I understand what is needed and wanted—the wedding, like any great production, is to be magical and meaningful, and the show is to go off without a hitch. No one must know about the work involved. Fortunately those heavy red velvet curtains hide the stage-hands and the frantic activity in the wings."

"You're the stage manager."

"I understand this is not my play or my production. I am simply there to make people happy."

"Very much like your mother then."

She felt a hot lance of shame. "Except I don't sleep with people to make them happy," she flashed, voice hardening.

"That's not what I meant."

"No? Then what did you mean?"

He regarded her from beneath heavy lids, his black lashes nearly concealing the piercing blue of his eyes. "I think you want to take offense. You've been harboring this resentment for years."

If she'd been anywhere else she would have bolted from her seat and raced away, but seeing as they were thirty thousand feet in the air on a small private jet, there was nowhere to go. No way to escape. "Resentment against what, and whom? I am not a victim, Marcu. I am satisfied with my life, pleased by what I have accomplished. Everything I own, and everything I've achieved, has been through hard work, not gifts, or handouts."

"I wasn't implying that you've slept with anyone to get where you are—"

"Good, because I haven't."

"All I was saying was that your mother's… success…was due to her ability to give people what they wanted."

"Can we not discuss my mother? We don't constantly reference your mother, and I know her absence wounded you."

His broad shoulders shifted carelessly. "At least I knew her. The younger ones have no memories of her."

"You were how old when she left?"

"Twelve."

"The same age I was when I arrived at your family's palazzo."

"Do you remember being twelve?"

"I do," she answered. "And you?"

"I do, too." His long fingers casually drummed on the leather armrest. "Mothers are important. It's why I must remarry."

"Do your children like Vittoria?"

"They've only met her a few times, but there were no problems, and Vittoria seemed quite taken with Antonio." He hesitated. "It's easier to adapt when the children are very young, and Antonio is little more than a toddler."

"How old are they?"

"Three, five, and nearly seven," he answered. "Antonio is my youngest, Rocca, my only girl, is five, and Matteo will be seven just after the New Year."

"Matteo, like your father."

"Yes."

She said nothing for a long moment, and it was then that Marcu filled the silence. "My father liked you, you know. He was always quite protective of you."

She'd always thought so, too, until that last night when he'd said such terrible, hurtful things to Marcu about her. *She is not the sort you get serious with. Remember her background. Remember who she is, and where she comes from. A dalliance is delightful, but she is not one you keep.*

And then Marcu's brutal reply: *Of course I know. I do not need the reminder. When I marry it will be to someone suitable.*

Marcu didn't know she'd inadvertently over-
heard the conversation. He hadn't even known
he'd wounded her, and yet even then, he'd been
more than happy to see her leave Palermo, buy-
ing her one-way airline ticket to London with
startling alacrity before driving her to the airport himself.

She'd been numb on the flight to London, and
she'd been numb as she collected her luggage
at Heathrow. The only thought circling her exhausted brain was that he couldn't wait to see
her gone, and he hadn't been able to get rid of
her fast enough. Their passionate night wasn't
meaningful at all to him. Instead it was a mistake. A colossal embarrassment.

As she searched for a place to live, Monet
consoled herself with the fact that at least they
hadn't consummated their lovemaking. At least
she'd only given him her heart, and not her innocence. It wasn't that she cherished her virginity, but she certainly didn't need to give Marcu
more than she already had.

Monet gave her head a faint shake and forced
her attention to the present. The next three
weeks would be difficult. She wasn't worried about the children, as she'd cared for chil-

dren in the past, but she dreaded even a few hours in close proximity to Marcu, never mind a few days, because memories were flooding her and the memories created pain. "He really gave your sisters pink robes for Christmas one year?"

"Yes."

"You don't think it was inappropriate for him to give me a satin bathrobe?"

"I am certain he didn't mean to make you uncomfortable. Knowing him, I'm positive he meant well."

She bit the inside of her lower lip to keep from contradicting him because if Matteo had meant well, he wouldn't have poisoned Marcu against her. He wouldn't have talked about her as if she was little more than garbage.

Marcu shot her a narrowed glance. "You don't believe me."

"I don't know what I believe anymore," she answered simply, and that was the truth.

Their private jet landed twenty-five minutes later at the executive airport in Milan, where Marcu's gleaming black Maserati was waiting. A steward stowed the luggage in the boot of the car and Marcu opened the passenger door for Monet. The interior of the new car was as sleekly designed as the exterior, the black leather plush, and still smelling new. They left the airport immediately for the drive to the *castello*, a drive that should take less than two hours if the weather was good, and the weather was good.

She and Marcu were mostly silent as he drove them up into the mountains. Snow blanketed the hills but the road was clear and free of ice. Monet struggled to relax but it was difficult in the close confines of the luxurious sports car. Everything about Marcu overwhelmed her— he was both familiar and not, changed by time and yet even more ruggedly appealing than before. She wanted to be indifferent to him but everything in her felt far too sensitive and aware of the way he sat, and the way his hand rested on the stick shift, and how his other hand looked against the black leather steering wheel. He had strong hands, beautiful hands. Just like his profile was strong, and beautiful. More chiseled and beautiful than it had been eight years ago.

"Do you have snow tires on the car?" she asked as Marcu took another sharp curve with ease.

"I do, and I also have chains if needed." He shot her a mocking glance from beneath dense black lashes. "Nervous?"

"No," she lied, crossing her legs.

"You're wringing your hands."

She unknotted her hands and smoothed her heather-gray skirt, then made a conscious decision to at least fake appearing relaxed, even if she didn't feel it on the inside.

Marcu wouldn't be around much longer. He'd be leaving for his holiday with Vittoria soon. It would just be her and the children by the end of the week, and she'd be fine with the kids. Even if they were little beasts, she'd be fine. She could manage just about anything...except her reaction to Marcu it seemed.

"I'm sorry we're arriving so late," he said. "It's a beautiful drive in daylight."

She turned her head to look out the window, the soaring peaks of the Alps hidden now by darkness. "I would imagine you have good views from your *castello*?"

"Breathtaking," he agreed.

And that was the end of their conversation until they reached the Aosta Valley, where Marcu's *castello* sat just outside the village of Aosta. She'd been many places in her life, but she'd never been to the Italian Alps and she was looking forward to exploring someplace new. Hopefully the children would have a sense of adventure, too.

"Here," Marcu said abruptly as they left the highway to turn off the main road, passing through huge iron gates and stone walls into a groomed winter wonderland. The road cut through the middle of an ancient park filled with soaring trees frosted with snow and just when Monet was certain they'd be driving through woods forever, the trees cleared and before them rose a castle. It could be called nothing else with its stone-and-stucco facade, and soaring towers and turrets.

"This isn't a new construction," she said under her breath.

His lips curved faintly. "It was built at the end of the twelfth century."

"So I'm sure it's warm and cozy inside."

"Fortunately, Galeta's family updated the

heating. We don't just rely on drafty fireplaces. And should you be cold at night, there are small space heaters you can plug in as well."

Marcu slowed as they traveled up a narrow cobbled road and then parked in front of the entrance to the *castello*. Staff appeared on the front steps. Men in dark gray suits claimed the luggage while a woman in an austere black dress nodded her head as Marcu ushered Monet through the front door. "Welcome back, Signor Uberto," the woman said.

"Thank you," Marcu answered. "Are the children still up?"

"No, *signor*, they are already in bed and asleep. The housemaid, Elise, took them for a walk to help them burn off their energy earlier and they were ready for bed tonight."

Monet heard the wryness in the housekeeper's voice and glanced from the housekeeper to Marcu to see how he'd interpret her words, but Marcu's stern features revealed nothing.

"Were they difficult to manage without Miss Sheldon?" he asked.

"Not at all, sir. Elise enjoys spending time with them."

"Tell her I'm grateful for her help," Marcu

instructed, tugging off his leather gloves and then his coat.

"She knows, *signor*. Do not worry."

The butler was there to take Marcu's coat, and then he turned to Monet, ready to collect hers, but she smiled and shook her head. "I'd like to keep mine, if I could," she said.

"Of course." Marcu glanced up the stairwell to the floors above. "I'll give you a quick tour now and then tomorrow you can have a proper look around."

"That's all right," Monet said quickly. "I don't need a tour tonight. It's been a long day and I'm happy to just call it a night. But I do look forward to meeting the children in the morning."

"Your suite of rooms is next to the nursery on the third floor," Marcu answered. "I'll walk you there."

They climbed three flights of stairs before Marcu opened the door on the third floor to a sitting room with a dark beamed ceiling.

The walls were a creamy plaster over stone. The pale stone floors were covered with plush Persian rugs, and a rich burgundy velvet couch faced the fireplace, with a pair of peach brocade upholstered chairs on either side. There were small tables scattered about, one round table topped with hand-painted burgundy-and-gold tiles, while another had a hammered silver tray that reminded her of a table they'd once had in Morocco. A Venetian glass mirror hung on one of the smooth plaster walls while an antique peach, green and gold tapestry hung on another.

"The children are next door," Marcu said. "Their nursery and bedrooms take up the rest of the floor. They have a playroom, and two bedrooms. Matteo and Antonio share a room, and Rocca has her own. Miss Sheldon used to sleep in the nursery in Palermo to be near them, but once Antonio turned three, we moved the boys in together and now Miss Sheldon has a bedroom adjacent to the nursery like here."

"If they have a bad dream, what do they do?"

"They know you're here, next door."

"They don't come to you?"

"You are closer. I'm on a floor below and the stairs are steep."

"I see," she said, careful to keep the judgment from her voice as she crossed the living-room carpet to peek through the open door to the bedroom. The apricot-and-burgundy color scheme was repeated. The bed was a four-poster with apricot fabric panels. Wooden shutters were at the windows but heavy curtains framed the shutters, adding an extra layer of protection against the frigid night temperature.

Marcu gestured to a large wardrobe in the corner. "You'll find a mini kitchen outfitted in the wardrobe with a coffeemaker, teakettle, and a small refrigerator. I believe housekeeping has stocked it with milk and some fruit and snacks. I know we had dinner on the plane, but if you're hungry for something more substantial—"

"I'm not," she said, cutting him off. "But thank you. I think I'll have a cup of tea and call it a night. I imagine the children will wake early and be ready to go."

"Elise will look after them until you're settled."

"I'm settled now," she said firmly.

"I'll send for you once they are up and dressed and fed. There is an intercom button inside the wardrobe, and another on the wall near your bedroom light switch. You can call the butler at any time—we have a night attendant available—and request food, drink, or anything else you might need."

"The children have one in their room, too?"

"Yes. But they don't use it. Normally they get Miss Sheldon and then she handles their requests."

A light knock sounded at the bedroom door. Marcu crossed to open her door. A castle steward was on the doorstep with Monet's luggage and silently entered the room, carrying her suitcase and smaller bag into the bedroom.

Marcu looked at her. "Any other questions?"

"No." She suddenly felt exhausted and disoriented. What *was* she doing here? "I'll wait for you to send for me tomorrow."

It took Marcu hours to fall asleep. He was too keyed up, too restless to switch his thoughts off so he could sleep.

Now that Monet was here he could focus on his trip with Vittoria. He'd already looked at rings in Milan and his assistant at the Palermo office had booked the top floor of the resort Altapura for him and Vittoria, as well as making several reservations at the best restaurants. Vittoria was far more extroverted than Galeta had been and she enjoyed the social scene. It was one of the reasons he was taking her to the Alps. She loved showing off her prowess on the slopes during the day, and she enjoyed dressing up at night. Christmas for her was about parties and people, and he was trying to muster enthusiasm for a holiday that sounded dreadful.

He didn't want to be away from the children. He didn't want to be in some damn hotel. And he didn't want to propose over Christmas—he hated this time of year—but Vittoria had made it clear that she wanted a commitment from him, and she wanted it by the New Year.

Vittoria wasn't the perfect solution to his wife problem, but she came from a well-respected family, an old, powerful, wealthy Sicilian family, and she was beautiful and outgoing, which he thought would be good for the children. Proposing to Vittoria wasn't an impulsive decision. They'd been seeing each other for the past year and she'd handled herself well when she'd been with his children. Of course the children were a little standoffish because they didn't yet know her, but they would grow to care for her, and Vittoria would care for them. With time, everything would fall into place.

The hard part was done. Details had been organized, and everything problematic was sorted. It hadn't been easy, but Monet was here now and she'd take care of things for the next few weeks while he was gone. The children would be fine. Vittoria would accept his proposal. There was no reason to worry.

And yet, sleep still eluded him.

All because Monet was here, just one floor above his.

CHAPTER FOUR

MONET WAS AWAKE long before her breakfast tray was delivered to her room along with a folded card.

The children and I will meet you in the music room at nine. The music room is one floor down, and the second door on the left.
Marcu

She'd already had two cups of tea and a biscotti when the breakfast tray of yogurt, juice, and warm fragrant rolls arrived. She'd thought she was hungry until she read the note and then her stomach did nervous flips.

She wasn't ready to see Marcu again. To be honest, she found him rather terrifying. There was no boy left in his handsome face, and no softness in his personality. The loss of his wife had hardened him and made him intimidating and ruthless.

Years ago she would have said he'd be an amazing father but now he struck her as impossibly cold. She hoped he wasn't truly that cold with his children.

One minute before nine she left her room, headed down the stone stairs and counted the doors on the left, opening the second door as instructed.

The music room looked like a formal sitting room with antique chairs and oil paintings on the walls. The baby grand piano near the tall leaded window was the only instrument in the room. On closer inspection Monet discovered that the oil painting hanging over the fireplace was of a young woman playing the harp, while the painting near the piano was of a man playing the violin. So she was in the right room—this had to be the music room—but where were Marcu and the children?

She glanced at her watch. It was a minute past nine now. Perhaps they were still at breakfast.

She walked to the piano and lightly ran her fingers over the keys, not pressing hard enough to create sound. The keys were smooth beneath her touch and she was tempted to sit down and play something—she'd never had formal lessons but she'd learned to play by ear—but wasn't sure if Marcu would frown on her playing the piano here. He'd once played the piano. He'd been a serious musician, taking lessons and practicing for an hour or more every day. At the palazzo she'd creep into a corner and listen to him practice, amazed by his gift. When he played, he made her feel so much. Maybe it was music that had made her fall in love with him.

"Sorry to be late," Marcu said in English, as he entered the room, looking sophisticated and impossibly masculine in a black turtleneck sweater and black wool trousers. He didn't wear the clothes, they wore him, hugging his broad shoulders and narrow waist, while outlining his muscular torso and thighs.

Heat washed through her, and Monet bit down into her lower lip, hating the sudden weakness she felt as Marcu ushered his three shy young children toward her.

The children all had dark glossy hair, but it was the smaller boy, the one who must be Antonio, that was the spitting image of Marcu. The resemblance was so strong it nearly made

Monet smile. *"Buongiorno,"* Monet said huskily in Italian. *Good morning.*

"These are my children," Marcu said, switching to Italian as he lined the children up by age. "Matteo, Rocca, and Antonio."

"It's nice to meet you," Monet said, approaching Matteo first and shaking his hand. "I am Monet."

"Signorina Wilde," Marcu corrected. "I can call you Monet because I have known you many years, but the children must call you Signorina." He clapped Matteo firmly on the shoulders. "And they will be good for you. They have promised to be obedient and polite and not make things difficult while you are here with them."

Marcu couldn't see how the little girl's face tightened, or how young Antonio blinked hard to hide the fact that his eyes were watering. She felt a pang of sympathy. The children were even more anxious about the change in their child care than she was. "I am only temporary," she reassured them. "Signorina Sheldon will be back before you know it."

"I have a great deal to attend to," Marcu said. "Can I leave them to you, Signorina Wilde?

You're welcome to stay here or go upstairs to the nursery. I'm certain the children will be happy to show you around."

"We're fine. Please, don't worry about us," Monet assured him, giving him a bright smile. "See you later."

"We'll all have dinner tonight," he answered, heading for the door. "I'll see you then."

After Marcu left the music room, there was just silence. The three children gazed at her, clearly uncertain, as well as more than a little curious.

It had been a long time since Monet had spoken Italian but she was sure it wouldn't take long for it to come back as it was a language she'd spoken daily for years. "Do any of you play?" Monet asked, pointing to the piano.

The children shook their heads.

"Mamma used to play," the little girl said. "This was her music room."

"Your father plays for you, doesn't he?"

They looked at each other, puzzled, before shaking their heads.

"He used to play really well," Monet said, but this was followed by more silence. Monet gazed back at the children, lips curved, uncertain as how to proceed. She remembered from her past work that if she was too friendly the children would think her weak, and someone to be ignored, but if she didn't appear somewhat friendly and kind, then they would fear the worst.

"Did you really use to live at our house?" the little girl, Rocca, asked after a moment.

"This one?" Monet asked. "No—"

"No, not here," Rocca said quickly. "This isn't our home, this is Nonno and Nonna's house. Our house is in Palermo."

"The palazzo?" Monet clarified.

The children nodded.

Monet sat down on the edge of one of the chairs upholstered in gold silk. "I did. I knew your father when I was much younger, and I spent six years at the palazzo. It's a very beautiful place to live, isn't it?"

"It's very old," Matteo said. "I like more modern houses."

Monet's eyebrows lifted. "Are you interested in design?"

"No, but you can't get good Wi-Fi in the palazzo, at least, not in parts of it," Matteo said mournfully. "And it's even worse here. Here there is no internet. I can't play games with my friends."

"But you won't be here forever, and then you'll be back in Palermo," Monet replied. "Surely there are fun things about being here. Tell me some of your favorite things to do."

For a moment no one said anything, and the children looked at each other before Matteo shrugged. "We mostly do nothing. Everyone is very busy."

"And what about your father?" Monet couldn't help asking the question.

"He is very busy with work," Matteo said with a sigh, sounding resigned.

"Papà is important," Antonio added forlornly. "Everybody needs him."

The three faces before her looked so woebegone that Monet immediately wondered how much of their father they actually did see. "Well, I hate sitting around doing nothing so the four of us will do lots of fun things. We will need to make a list." Monet glanced from one young face to another, not certain why they weren't more enthused. "I would think this is a magical place to spend Christmas."

"Maybe," Matteo said, shoulders shrugging.

"We used to come in summer. This is the first time we've come for Christmas."

Monet hid her surprise. From the way Marcu had described taking her to the children in the Alpine *castello*, one would have thought this was their annual tradition. "I didn't realize. I thought you came here every year."

"No. But Papà says it's going to be a different Christmas this year," Rocca said, before glancing at her brothers. "We don't know what that means."

Monet felt a heavy, sinking sensation in her chest. Had Marcu not yet told them that he was leaving them for the Christmas holidays? But she couldn't bear to think of that, not yet. "When were you last here? In the summer?"

"No. It's been a long time," Matteo said.

"I didn't even remember it," Rocca said.

"Me, either," Antonio said.

"That's because you've never been here before," Matteo said to Antonio before glancing at Monet.

"Papà didn't want to come here after Mamma died. It was her house. We inherited it when Nonno and Nonna died. They are all gone now."

"Inherited means it's ours now," Rocca said gravely.

Monet folded her hands. "It must be very hard for you, not having your mother."

There was a beat of silence. "We don't remember her very much," Rocca answered. "I should because I'm five, but it's been too long. Papà says she loved us."

"I am sure she did." Monet scooted over in the upholstered chair and patted the golden silk cushion. "Won't you tell me about her? The parts that you remember... Or the parts that you have been told?"

"She was beautiful," the little girl said, taking a seat on the couch but leaving space between her and Monet. "I look like her. Papà said we have the same eyes, and the same nose and smile. There are pictures of her in the gallery. We can show them to you."

"Oh, I'd like that very much," Monet answered. "Could we do that now? I'd love to explore your *castello*. It's very big and I'm afraid without your help I'll get lost."

The children escorted her down the long corridor lined with ancestral portraits. Monet half smiled at the portraits, nearly all with long hair, black curls on both the men and women, and lots of velvet and ruffles, along with rings and necklaces, brooches and headbands, but what was one to expect when the family in question dated back centuries?

As the children led the way down the hall, the portraits became more modern, and the clothing became contemporary, until at last they came to a gold-framed oil of an elegant young woman with dark blond hair and wide brown eyes. She had a pale, creamy complexion, high cheekbones and a long aquiline nose. Her honey-colored hair was drawn back and her expression was rather aloof, and Monet wondered if that was really her personality or if the portrait painter had chosen that cool, detached expression for her.

"Mamma," Antonio announced.

"She is very lovely," Monet said. "I just wish she was smiling here. I'd love to know if she had a dimple like Rocca's."

"She didn't," Marcu said decisively, his deep voice coming from behind them.

Monet hadn't realized he'd joined them in the corridor and she stiffened in surprise, wondering how long he'd been standing there listening to them.

She glanced over her shoulder at him, her gaze again taking in his soft turtleneck and the well-tailored black trousers. He looked incredibly physically fit, as well as handsome and wealthy and altogether too powerful, which made her pulse race, and her stomach tighten with knots of apprehension, but also knots of something else.

She didn't want to contemplate the something else.

She wasn't here for something else.

He'd essentially forced her to come do a job so that he could be with yet another woman that wasn't her. She shouldn't respond to him. And she most definitely shouldn't care for him. After all these years, she shouldn't care that she wasn't the right woman for him and that she would never be the right one, and yet still, it stung. She didn't know if it was her pride, or that something else, but the fact that he could so easily dismiss her as someone valuable, and worthy of being kept and cherished, still made her ache.

She turned away as he approached, focusing

instead on the children's faces, curious to see how they'd respond to his surprise visit. They didn't rush toward him, but then, Marcu and his brother and sisters hadn't rushed toward their father, either. They'd always greeted each other with kindness and civility, but control and discipline were always evident, just as they were now.

"I'm surprised you are still on this floor of the *castello*. You haven't made it very far in your tour," Marcu said.

"We have weeks to discover everything," Monet said lightly. "It's nice just to chat and get to know each other." She looked at him. "And I thought we weren't going to see you until dinner. Have you decided to join our tour?"

"My office is on the other side of that wall. I'm finding it difficult concentrating with all the chatter."

Monet saw Rocca's expression fall and it made her angry. Marcu seemed determined to disappoint his children. "Or maybe you were hoping to join us on our tour." She looked at the children. "Where should we go next?"

"The ballroom!" Rocca said.

"We're going to the ballroom," Monet said to

Marcu with an arch of one eyebrow. "Would you care to join us?"

Rocca glanced up at him hopefully but he gave a swift decisive shake of his head. "I have too much work to do," he said.

Again Monet felt a wash of anger. Did he really have that much work to do? Or was he simply avoiding his children? It seemed to her, from all he'd told her, that he wanted as little to do with them as possible. It made no sense. Marcu had once been the most loving, considerate, and selfless of all the Ubertos. He'd been so patient with his younger brother and sisters, generous with his time, always available for a game or to listen and give a bit of advice.

"You're smart not to go with us," Monet flashed back, giving him a sunny smile. "We're going to the ballroom to dance. So, no waltzes for you, Signor Uberto."

"I'd prefer the children to go outside for their morning walk," Marcu said.

"Is that what they usually do, *signor*?"

"Yes. Exercise every morning after breakfast."

"Is there a certain number of push-ups they are to do, too?" she retorted.

He growled something indecipherable under his breath. "Don't challenge me," he said in English, "and never in front of them."

"Why don't you join us for a bit? You can tell me your rules and expectations that way."

"The children know."

She bit back her protest. He might still be gorgeous but he'd become incredibly unlikable. She executed a quick curtsy. "Very well, sir. Have a good day, sir."

"Monet." His voice held a hint of warning.

She stepped closer to him, and dropped her voice, ensuring that the children wouldn't hear as she replied in hushed English. "I've only been here a few hours, Marcu, but it seems to me that the children don't need a new mother, but rather they need a new father."

His hand reached out to clasp her arm. "Not acceptable."

She lifted her chin and her eyes met his. "Don't like it? Fire me."

"That's what you want, isn't it?"

"No, what I want is the kind Marcu. The one that loved his family and didn't punish them for loving him." Their gazes locked and held, his blue eyes glittering with anger. He was beautiful and cold and frightening, but she was just as tough, and just as fierce, and she wasn't going to let him intimidate her. He was the one who demanded she come here. He claimed he needed help—her help. Well then, he was going to get it, whether he liked it or not.

Suddenly the hard pressure of his hand wrapped around her arm eased. A shadow darkened his eyes. "I'm not a monster."

"No? Then don't act like one," she said as his hand dropped. Her arm tingled from his touch, but she ignored the crazy sensations ricocheting through her and turned to the children, holding out a hand to Rocca, and then to Antonio. "Lead the way. I'm anxious to see what a ballroom would look like in this magnificent *castello*."

The children obliged, walking her out of the picture gallery, and down two floors, through the main entrance of the house, and down a side corridor, where they passed through a stone archway into a stunning room with a gold-stenciled ceiling and fresco-covered walls. The floor featured a marble parquet pattern and three enormous chandeliers lined the ceiling and tall windows filled the room with sunlight.

"Ooh, this is beautiful," Monet said. "I have a feeling this room has hosted some glorious parties, don't you think?"

"Mamma's coming-out ball was in this room," Rocca said proudly. "And Nonno's mother's ball, too. Papà said the balls are usually in the summer because the weather is so beautiful then."

"Well, I think this is beautiful any time of year," Monet answered. "But maybe we should fetch your coats and get some fresh air. It's sunny and beautiful right now."

"And cold," Rocca said. "I miss Sicily."

"You'll be back to Sicily before you know it," Monet countered cheerfully, "which is why you should make the most of your visit here while you can. What could we do later after we go for a walk? Is there anything you've been wanting to do?"

The children glanced at each other and shook their heads.

Monet led them from the ballroom so they could head upstairs to change for their walk. "What about the Christmas market?" she asked. "The Marché Vert Noël in Aosta is supposed to be one of the best in Italy."

"I don't think we can go," Matteo said gruffly as they reached the second floor.

"Why not?" Monet asked, pausing on the landing to wait for Antonio to catch up. "There's delicious food, and bands that play music at night. We could look at the handicrafts and sample sweets."

Rocca scrunched her nose. "We'd have to get permission from Papà and he only ever says yes to us walking and hiking and doing sporty things. He believes the two best things for us are reading and exercise." She huffed a breath. "I hate it, though."

"Reading and exercise?" Monet asked.

"Yes, because I can't read very good yet, and Antonio can't read at all. He doesn't even know most of his letters."

"But he will when he's older. You will all be excellent readers," Monet said, "because reading is fun—"

"Papà says life isn't mean to be fun," Matteo interrupted. "Life is serious, which is why we must be serious, too."

Monet had to hold her breath to keep her frustration in, and it crossed her mind as they reached the nursery door that maybe she really was needed here for Christmas, and the reason had nothing to do with Marcu needing a wife, but everything to do with Marcu embracing his children.

Although they were all to have dinner together that night, Marcu couldn't join them at the last minute and Monet had dinner with the children in the dining room. They'd finished the meal and were now enjoying their dessert, a delicious *budino* with salted caramel, and the children were happily dipping their spoons into the custard layer topped with a salty-sweet caramel sauce.

"I did some reading while you were reading this afternoon and I discovered that during the Middle Ages, this valley was one of the main passages through the Alps, and you couldn't pass through without paying a toll, which gave those who lived here power and money," Monet said, reaching for her coffee. "Castles like this one were built overlooking the valley so the nobleman could see who was approaching, and then he could stop the traveler and demand a toll. Savvy nobles could earn a lot of money monitoring traffic in and out of the valley."

"Our *castello* is really old," Antonio said, licking his spoon. "So old."

"It was built around the original square tower," Matteo said. "You can see the tower if you look carefully. Rooms were added to the tower to create more living space."

Suddenly Marcu was there in the dining room with them, drawing his chair out at the end of the table and taking a seat. "Not just living space," he said, "but public space for conducting government business. The ballroom you visited today was originally a public meeting room, where the locals could come petition the nobleman for help."

Surprised, but also pleased by Marcu's appearance, Monet bit her lip and let him take over the conversation.

"Where can you see the original tower?" Marcu asked his children.

"The kitchen," Matteo said promptly, "because it's all stone, everywhere, and the walls are very thick."

"The main entrance," Rocca said, smiling shyly at her father.

"Your study," Matteo added, "your bedroom and then the *signorina*'s bedroom. They all have the same beamed ceilings, fireplaces, and windows, too."

"That's right," Marcu said, before thanking the steward who'd appeared almost immediately with a coffee and dessert for him. "You can tell the original tower from the newer additions by the change in building material, as well as the thickness of the walls and how the windows are placed within the wall." He paused and glanced at his children, and then at Monet. "Did you have a good day today?"

The children nodded.

"What did you do?"

Monet noticed the children weren't in a hurry to answer so she gave a quick recap of their day. "We walked a lot, and went to the village to look at the Roman theater, and then we came back for lunch, and read, and played games." She lifted her coffee cup and gazed at Marcu over the rim, finding it impossible to look at anyone but him. Marcu had always been fit, but he was downright virile now. She wished he wasn't so appealing. She wished she could sit here and feel nothing. Instead she sat here and felt everything.

Thank God she'd grown up these past eight

years. She might still be physically attracted to him, and she might still be awash in emotions, but at least the past eight years had taught her self-control, and discipline. She would never let him know how she felt, unwilling to let her emotions or her inexperience make a difficult situation impossible. "What about you?" she said with a faint smile. "How was your day, Signor Uberto?"

"A busy day," he answered in Italian. "I had a very full schedule of calls and meetings."

"The world markets never sleep, do they?"

"No. And the New York Stock Exchange is proving to be very volatile this week, requiring extra calls and consultations." His gaze swept the children, who were beginning to droop, and he switched to English. "They're looking tired."

"I think it's your mention of the stock market. It's enough to put anyone to sleep."

"Unless you're a financier or economist."

She glanced at the children. The custard desserts were gone, or nearly gone, but they'd stopped eating. Antonio's shoulders slumped and he was yawning broadly. "They do look sleepy," she said, "but I hate taking them away now. You've only just arrived."

"They're used to it."

"That's not a good thing, Marcu—" She broke off, flustered to have slipped and used his first name in front of the children. "I'm sorry. I meant, Signor—"

"You can call me Marcu. It's uncomfortable hearing you call me 'mister' and 'sir.'"

"But Miss Sheldon…?"

"She's my employee. You're…" His voice faded. He frowned and gave his head a sharp shake. "I don't know what you are."

Monet flushed, growing warm all over. Her cheeks suddenly felt too hot, and her skin too sensitive. "A friend of the family?"

"Yes," he said gruffly. "That would work." And yet there was an indecipherable emotion in his eyes that made her feel as if he was saying something altogether different.

"It's late," he said abruptly, rising and abandoning his coffee and dessert. "You should take the children up before they fall asleep in their custard cups."

"Of course." Monet rose from the table. "Come, my lovelies," she said to the children. "Let me walk you up and we'll get ready for bed."

The children kissed their father good-night and then Marcu added as she reached the doorway, "When you've finished putting them to bed, please come join me back downstairs in the smaller of the drawing rooms. I'd like to discuss my travel plans with you."

CHAPTER FIVE

MONET HATED THAT her pulse quickened as she headed down the stairs to meet Marcu in the drawing room. She hated that butterflies filled her middle even as she fought down a sense of excitement and expectancy. She shouldn't be feeling excited, or expectant. What did she think would happen? What was she hoping would happen? Ridiculous. This whole thing was beyond ridiculous. She was beyond ridiculous.

One of the housemaids had told her where to find the drawing room that Marcu favored for the evenings and she quietly opened the door and spotted him sitting in a chair near the fire reading from his stack of papers.

He looked up as she entered the room. "They are in bed?" he asked.

She nodded. "All sleeping soundly."

"Was it difficult?" he asked, folding the newspaper and adding it to the pile at his elbow. "It was your first time putting them to bed."

"They were talkative at first, so I let them talk and then I told them a story, and then we said prayers, and they fell asleep."

"They are in two separate bedrooms—did you tell two separate stories?"

"I brought them together for the stories and then we said the prayers together before I tucked each into his or her own bed."

"There wasn't a lot of resistance?"

"Is there usually?"

He hesitated. "When I put them to bed, yes."

Monet clasped her hands in front of her, feeling rather like a governess in a historical novel being called to explain her actions to her employer. She didn't like the feeling. She didn't like having to answer to Marcu. "May I sit?" she asked, "Or does Miss Sheldon not sit when asked to present herself to you?"

Marcu stared at her a long moment before the corner of his mouth lifted in a faint, wry smile. "You are not Miss Sheldon."

"No, I'm not."

"Please sit. Anywhere you like."

She glanced at her choices and saw that there

were overstuffed armchairs near his, next to the fire, and then another seating area at the opposite end of the room. She obviously couldn't go sit at the far end of the room so she took one of the upholstered chairs by the fire. The fabric was soft, the cushions comfortable. She immediately felt better. "I could tell you why I think the children don't want to go to sleep when you put them to bed, but maybe you don't want to hear my opinions."

"You've only been here one day," he said mildly.

"I know, but I've had a lot of time today to think about what I've seen and heard, and I think the reason they are resistant to being put to bed when you do it is that they want more time with you, and they're not ready to let you go."

He was silent a moment before he shrugged his broad shoulders. "I love them and yet I can't give them everything they need. It feels like a losing battle. No matter what I do, it will never be enough."

"They don't require your soul. They do want your time, they want consistency, and they want love."

"You can say that because you have no children of your own."

"True. I don't have any of the guilt or anxiety you have. I have a job to do, and I know what I need to do. If I am doing my job to the best of my ability then I don't rake myself over the coals. There would be no point in that."

He got to his feet and glanced at the fire, and then her. "Would you like a drink? Sherry or maybe a glass of port?"

She started to shake her head, and then thought yes, she really would love something to drink. She could use a drink tonight. The children had not been difficult for her and yet it was still a long day, a tiring day, and she could feel the ache of tension in her back. "That would be lovely."

She watched as he crossed the room, going to a table against the wall with crystal decanters and bottles with pretty labels. He was still wearing his black wool trousers and the cashmere sweater that lovingly wrapped his muscular chest and biceps. His skin was burnished and his black hair looked glossy in the overhead light and she was fascinated by each of his movements as he reached for one of the liqueur bottles, then a small glass, which he filled for her.

"I think you will like this," he said, before filling a glass for himself and carrying their drinks back to where she sat by the fire.

His fingers brushed hers as he handed her the small glass. She felt a leap of warmth at the simple touch, and something electric jolted through her, making her heart do a painful double beat. Panicked that she was too open and transparent, Monet dropped her head and inhaled the port's sweet rich fragrance. Cherries and chocolate and sunbaked fruit.

One sip of the rich spicy sweet port and she flashed back to early years in Morocco, and then with another sip, she flashed back to a summer spent outside Taormina with Marcu and his family. His father had rented an enormous marble villa just above the water. The house had an even bigger pool. She'd spent every day, all day, in the pool, or on a chaise-longue chair, soaking up the sun. It had been a blissful summer for a thirteen-year-old girl, especially as Marcu had joined them for three weeks and he'd been like a god to her—bronzed, muscular, handsome, charming. She couldn't look at him without feeling love and longing. He spoke carelessly of the girls he dated, girls he took on motorbikes for rides, girls he took out to special romantic dinners. She'd wanted to be one of those beautiful girls he took out at night on his motorbike. She'd wanted to be his girl and there was a time she would have given anything to make that dream come true.

The heat from the port mingled with the bruised sensation in her chest. There was nothing good about remembering the past. Nothing good would come from looking back. She couldn't do this...not to him, or herself.

"So Vittoria," Monet said, forcing her mind to the present. "How did you meet? What are the juicy details?" she asked, deliberately keeping her tone light and teasing.

He arched a black brow as he dropped back into his chair by the fire. "There are no juicy details. It's a rather businesslike proposition. I'm marrying for the children's sake, and so it's a practical arrangement rather than a romantic one."

Her brow creased. She hesitated. "So you don't...love her?"

"We both have a strong feeling of regard for each other."

"What does that even mean?"

"It means there is affection, and attraction, as well as respect for each other's families."

"That sounds dreadful. I pity her, and I pity you. To go from loving Galeta to a marriage of, well, convenience, it's horrible. You're short-changing Vittoria and yourself."

"It was no different with Galeta. It was the same sort of marriage, except that time there was the understanding that children were important and her number-one responsibility was to provide children. Which she did," he added flatly.

"So Vittoria's number-one responsibility is to take care of the children Galeta gave you."

He gazed at her steadily. "Is there a question in there?"

She felt a pang for him, and the man she remembered, because Marcu had been lovely... warm, kind, smart, witty. She missed him, because that was the man his children needed for a father, not the man he'd become.

"I wish I could say that I was amazed that women sign up for this life," she said carefully, "but we both know women do. My mother would have loved to have married a wealthy man. Instead she spent her life as the side piece, and perhaps she thought she had power that way, or some form of independence, but we both know she didn't. She was utterly dependent on the men that sought her out. Her acting jobs disappeared as she grew older and eventually she had no income other than what men like your father provided."

"My father took care of her until the day she died."

"She only lived another year after they broke up." Monet exhaled hard, and closed her eyes, aware of the rapid staccato of her heart. She hated that he could arouse her emotions so easily. She hated that they were connected through their parents' relationship. "I'm sorry. I shouldn't have said any of that, and you didn't invite me here to discuss your relationship with Vittoria, or our parents. I'm here to be instructed in my duties, and your travel plans."

He grimaced. "You're suddenly more formal than my very formal Miss Sheldon."

"As I should be. I'm here to help you manage things, not complicate matters. So tell me, what is your travel schedule? When will you leave? What should I know?"

"I'm leaving the day after tomorrow for a meeting in Palermo, followed by an overnight in Rome and then I should be back Thursday."

"That's a great deal of driving, or will you be flying?"

"My helicopter will arrive in Aosta helipad tomorrow afternoon, and once the sun is up, we'll be gone early Wednesday morning. If the weather holds, I'll be back late afternoon Thursday by helicopter. If the weather turns, I'll drive up from Milan. But I'll use my helicopter rather than my jet for this trip as I can land right at the palazzo and also on top of the Uberto Financial office tower in Rome. Saves a great deal of time not needing a runway."

"So we should plan for your return on Thursday."

"Yes. I'd like to have a day here with the children before I travel back to Rome Friday afternoon to pick up Vittoria for our holiday."

Monet held her breath, wanting to tell him that he wasn't even giving his children twenty-four hours before leaving again. Instead she inclined her head to show she understood. She had to be careful not to overstep, much less challenge him on every aspect of his parenting. These were not her children. This was but a temporary job for her.

And yet despite her best effort to bite her tongue she must have revealed something of her thoughts because Marcu's brow creased and he sat forward in his chair. "What have I said now?"

"It doesn't matter."

"But it does. I'd like to understand. I need to understand. Once I understood you."

That made her flinch, and she stiffened. "No," she said, quietly contradicting him. "You didn't understand me. You just thought you did."

His jaw tightened and his eyes narrowed. "I knew you better than anyone in my family."

"But that doesn't mean anything. Because if you'd truly known me, you wouldn't have—" She broke off and pressed her lips together, fighting all the recriminations that were bubbling up. Being near him had thrown the door open on the past and she was finding it impossible to live in the past and the present at the same time. It didn't work. She couldn't bear all the anger and pain. Anger was toxic. Pain created fresh pain. These emotions made her feel once again like the odd little girl with the odd mother with no home of their own.

"I wouldn't have what?" he finished for her.

She shook her head, determined to say no more. Determined to move forward. Determined to get through the next few weeks so she could be done with Marcu Uberto forever. "It's been a long day," she said, folding her hands together. "I'd like to get some sleep so I'll be rested for my day with the children tomorrow."

"Of course." He rose.

She rose, too. "Will we see you in the morning?"

"Probably not, but we'll have dinner together."

"I won't say anything about dinner with you to the children, so they won't be disappointed if it doesn't happen. It's better to not get their hopes up."

Heat flared in his eyes. "Is that a reprimand?"

"No, it's a statement of fact. Why make them promises that won't be kept? I think it's better to keep expectations low at this point."

"I have done my best."

"In this instance your best isn't good enough."

He closed the distance between them. "You

don't know what it was like, losing Galeta, being left with a newborn and two young children. It changed everything. It changed me."

"So I see, but as someone who was once your friend, they need more from you than a surrogate mother. Marcu, they need you. They need you to care—"

"I care!"

"Then don't leave them for Christmas. Stay—"

"Vittoria wants a Christmas proposal. She's made it clear she's expecting a Christmas proposal."

"Then bring her here. Have a family Christmas with her here."

"We will return, after the trip, and it's just one Christmas. It's only this year—"

"What if she demands you go skiing with her every Christmas? What if she wants to have a romantic Christmas with just the two of you every year?"

"She wouldn't."

"Are you sure? What do you really know about her? How do you know she will love them? You've introduced her to them, but there is no relationship, no bond, nothing to reassure you that she'll give them the tenderness they need."

"You have no children. What makes you an expert?"

"Because I know what it's like to constantly play second fiddle to your parents' romantic relationships. It hurts, Marcu."

Her voice cracked and the sheen of tears in her eyes made him want to rage against the injustice of the universe, because fate was harsh and life could be brutal and the only way to survive was by being hard. "Can't you see that I'm trying," he said, wrapping an arm around her back, holding her securely.

She blinked as she looked at him, cheeks flushed, eyes brilliant with fierce tears. "Are you?" she demanded. "Or are you hiding from them?"

"What does that mean?"

"The children don't even know you can play the piano. They don't know you love music and art and beauty—"

"I did. I don't anymore."

"Pity, because everyone needs beauty and art in their life. Children need beauty—"

"Why? It's just going to be snatched away."

"Beauty helps us through times of pain. Beauty, like love, heals and redeems—"

"I am certain there is plenty more you'd like to say," he growled, "but I've heard enough from you for one night."

His head descended and his lips covered hers. Monet stiffened with surprise, and panic, but the panic faded the second his lips touched hers.

Monet felt yanked back in time the moment she'd felt his arm circle her, his body pressing against hers, his frame lean and hard and so very male.

The brush of his lips and scent of his skin overwhelmed her with longing, and memory, and she was eighteen again, and in Marcu's spacious, luxurious bedroom suite at the Uberto palazzo. As the Uberto heir, he had the largest suite after his parents, gorgeous rooms that seemed to go on and on—living room, study, bedroom, en-suite bathroom, huge walk-in closet. He'd first kissed her in the doorway between his living room and study, and then they'd ended up on his bed, his large body pinning hers, their hands clasped, fingers entwined, her body arching against his, desperate for him.

This kiss eight years later flamed hot, and desperate. It was as if they had left off exactly where they'd stopped...the emotion, the need, the craving, so fierce, so insistent, and yet, so punishing. She had wanted him then, and she wanted him now, but want wasn't an easy thing, not with their history. The want created pain and anger, because he didn't care about her, not really. He desired her, the same way his father had desired her mother, but the Uberto men took different women to be their wives. They chose different women to be the mothers of their children. Rage and hurt welled within her, making her burn hot and cold. He'd make love to Monet tonight but then fly out tomorrow to propose to Vittoria.

She'd never be anything more than a side piece. Something used to satisfy one's carnal desire. Heartsick, she pushed against Marcu's chest, hard enough to free herself. He, too, was breathing heavily as his arms dropped, but he didn't move away. She took a frantic step backward, pulse racing, body trembling, even as something inside of her urged her to return to his arms, return to his warmth.

My God, she was stupid. She hadn't matured at all. He was still so dangerous and destructive, at least to her heart, never mind her self-control. She shot him a fierce look before leaving the study, fleeing for the privacy of her own room.

Marcu was as shocked as she was. He heard, rather than saw, Monet leave, even though his gaze followed her to the door, but he couldn't see as much as feel.

He felt stunned, his body hot and cold, but also, strangely alive. Energy coursed through him, hot primitive desire pumped through his veins. His muscles contracted, his heart thudded.

He wanted her.

He wanted her more than he'd ever wanted anyone.

Why?

Was it because she was forbidden? Was it because she represented youth and the last of his innocence?

Why did he crave her when he had never craved any other woman...ever?

His gaze lingered on the closed door, aware of how still everything had become. The room suddenly felt empty and cold without Monet.

He felt empty, and cold, but not as cold as he usually did. She'd lit a flame inside of him and the small flickering flame had the potential to burn brightly. If he let it.

He couldn't let it.

He couldn't give in to sensation, or emotion, or impulse. Not when he'd spent the past three years teaching his children that life wasn't about fun or pleasure. It was about duty, and discipline. It was about reason and intellect.

The flame inside of him was the opposite of logic. The flame was passion and fire and hunger, and it couldn't be allowed to burn. He had to snuff it out. He had to remember the lessons he'd been teaching the children. Order. Predictability. Self-control. These were the virtues and values he respected, and this is why he structured their world as he did. It was a conscious attempt to protect them from chaos. He believed that discipline and control would serve them well as they grew into adulthood. Discipline and control would allow them to make good decisions, logical decisions, so they wouldn't be disappointed by life, or worse, hurt by it.

He'd been hurt, repeatedly, until he'd finally learned what life was trying to teach him: emotions were not to be trusted, whereas a cool head, and sharp intellect, prevailed. Which is why he didn't teach his children about hope, or faith, and why he wasn't looking for love in marriage. He'd been brought up to believe that love was somehow redemptive. It wasn't. Everything he'd been taught was a lie. His childhood was one fabrication on top of another, and after Galeta's death, Marcu had resolved to parent differently. His children would be guided by knowledge and truth, and that was all.

Kissing Monet had been a terrible mistake and it wouldn't happen again.

CHAPTER SIX

GOOD GOD, WHAT had happened downstairs?

Monet frantically paced her private sitting room, her steps muffled by the thick peach-and-cream Persian rug, the peach and cream echoed in the glamorous Italian silk curtains at the windows and the apricot silk panels on the four-poster bed in the adjacent room.

She couldn't believe she'd let him kiss her. She couldn't believe she'd kissed him back, because she had, she most definitely had.

Horrified, she went into the bedroom to stare at her face in the Venetian mirror hanging above the dressing table. Her cheeks were flushed and her eyes looked feverishly bright. Her full mouth looked plump and very kissed... because she had been *very* kissed.

She pressed a hand to her lips, feeling the warmth and sensitivity, thinking it had been forever since she'd felt anything so good, or felt so alive.

She'd wanted the kiss, too. How she'd wanted it. There was no way she could blame him for reaching for her because she'd spent the past few days wondering what it would be like to kiss him now...and if his kiss could wreck her the way it had upended her world eight years ago.

For the past eight years she'd wondered if his kiss had been as overwhelming and wonderful as she remembered, or if it had simply been the fact that it was her first real kiss, and in her inexperience she'd made it out to be more than it was.

Eight years ago his kiss had stripped her bare, stealing her heart, making her his, and all this time she'd wondered why he had so devastated her. And now she knew. It wasn't inexperience. It wasn't innocence. It was *him*. There was something powerful, something electric, in his touch.

His lips on hers just now had made her feel so many things, awakening the past, as well as jolting her from complacency. She wasn't immune to him. She wasn't in control of herself here. She wasn't confident, either. From the time she arrived at the *castello* she'd been certain he was as aware of her as she was of him, and it wasn't a casual awareness, but the taut, aching awareness of heat and memory and barely suppressed desire.

The kiss downstairs had burned with desire. The kiss downstairs—

A firm knock sounded before the door to her outer room opened. Monet moved from the dressing table to the middle of her bedroom and Marcu was there, closing the door and holding a finger to his lips.

"Let's not have the children in here as well," he said tersely, his gaze sweeping her cozy sitting room with the beamed ceiling and stone fireplace.

"I don't recall inviting you in," she said.

"I wouldn't have had to chase you down in here, if you had stayed downstairs so we could have had a conversation—"

"There's nothing to discuss." Her teeth chattered slightly and she felt cold and hot all over again. She longed for a thick sweater, or blanket, to wrap herself in. She wanted to hide. She wanted to savor the kiss because she knew it would never happen again. It couldn't happen again. "We both know it was inappropriate."

"Yes. You're right. The kiss *was* inappropriate, which is why we must talk, because I can't propose to Vittoria, not if I'm kissing you."

His words sent a shudder through her. She needed him to propose to Vittoria so she could escape Marcu and the *castello*. "I can forgive the kiss if it doesn't happen again," she said quietly.

"It was a mistake."

"It absolutely was."

His blue gaze skewered her, burning all the way through her. "And I won't kiss you, or touch you again—"

"Good."

"—while I'm pursuing another relationship."

"Exactly."

"But should I choose to pursue a relationship with you, it's a different story."

Monet froze, and blinked, dumbfounded. *What had he just said?* "You're about to propose to Vittoria," she said unsteadily. "Let's not confuse things, shall we?"

"I'm looking for a mother for my children. That is my goal."

"I understand that, and I also understand that when you're in Rome Wednesday night, you'll be with Vittoria, and then again with her on Friday, and I want you to go knowing that things will be calm and happy here. I can assure you the children will be safe with me."

"I have no doubt. My children seem happy with you."

"Good. So from now on focus on Vittoria and I will focus on the children and we won't need to speak of this again as we both have agreed it's a mistake."

"Yes."

"And we're both agreeing now that it will not happen again. There will be no further contact between us, and no physical intimacy." She hesitated. "Will you tell her what happened? Will you tell her about the kiss?"

He didn't answer immediately, then he nodded abruptly. "I should, yes." And then he walked out, leaving her even more shaken then before.

Kissing Marcu had been a horrendous mistake and the memory of his warmth and touch and taste haunted her all night, making sleep almost impossible. Every time she began dreaming, it was of him, and being in his arms and in his bed and completing what had begun between them so many years ago.

By the time morning came, Monet was exhausted and tense and wishing she was back in London, in the safety of her flat. She wasn't safe here—not because Marcu would force himself on her, but because she didn't trust herself anymore. Not with him.

That kiss last night…

That kiss had stirred something dark and dangerous and altogether too unpredictable awake within her, making her feel things she didn't want to feel, things she'd only ever felt with Marcu.

He needed to go. He needed to leave Aosta as soon as possible and settle things with Vittoria so she could leave the Italian Alps, too. London had never been so appealing.

Midmorning, Monet and the children walked to Aosta village again, the children's snow boots tramping snow and crunching ice as they talked about nothing and everything. Their chatter made Monet smile because it was sweet and they were so kind to each other. Marcu might be strict and distant but his children were definitely loving.

"Oh, there's the Christmas market again," Rocca said, pointing to the stands and booths in the middle of the Roman theater. "I really do wish we could visit it."

"I'll ask your father," Monet answered.

"I don't think that's a good idea," Matteo said. "He will just say we can't come to town anymore and I like coming here."

"Why won't he approve?" Monet persisted.

"Because he doesn't like Christmas," Rocca said bluntly. "It makes him mad. He thinks it's better to not make such a fuss at this time of year, and focus instead on winter sports."

Monet tugged on her gloves, pulling them higher. "Is that why the *castello* isn't festive? I've noticed there are no decorations, no Christmas tree."

"We don't *ever* have a Christmas tree," Rocca added.

"Not even in Palermo?" she clarified, and was dismayed when the children shook their heads. This didn't make sense. In Palermo, at the palazzo, Christmas was important, special. In the six years she had spent in Sicily, the Uberto family celebrated Christmas in a big way, kicking off the season on December eighth when family and staff came together to decorate the house. The Uberto family celebrated both Italian and Sicilian traditions, and it was the highlight of the year.

"Since when?" she asked. "Because when I was living with your father's family in Palermo we most definitely celebrated Christmas. Your grandfather Matteo adored Christmas. It was his favorite time of year."

The children just shrugged and gave each other swift glances, but this time Monet saw the worry, and the secret they were keeping. "What are you not telling me? I can see it in your eyes, and your faces. You're not very good liars—which I might add is a good thing—so come on, tell me. You can trust me. Remember, I've known your father for many, many years. Why don't you have a tree and do festive things?"

"It's because this is when my *mamma* died," Rocca blurted.

Matteo nodded grimly. "She died December sixteenth."

"After Antonio was born," Rocca added.

"Me," Antonio chimed in.

December sixteenth had been yesterday. Galeta had died three years ago yesterday.

Monet held her breath, overwhelmed. "Antonio, you must have just had a birthday," she said.

"Last week," Rocca answered for him, giving her brother a little pat.

Monet's heart went out to the children. So much had happened in their lives. There had been so much loss and pain. And then she thought of Marcu, and their conversation last night, and she understood him a little better, understood his pain and desperation better. For three years he'd been grieving and he was desperate for the grief to end. He was desperate for some kind of normalcy for his children, even if he was going about it the wrong way.

"It's cold," Rocca said, clapping her hands.

"Let's keep walking," Monet said, "before you turn to icicles."

Antonio laughed and took Monet's hand but Matteo walked ahead, shoulders hunched. Monet let him walk ahead for a while and then stopped him as they neared the village. "What are you thinking about?"

"I remember when we did have a Christmas tree," he said quietly. "We still do have a *presepi*, but it's not out yet. Maybe we didn't bring it from home."

Monet knew the *presepi*, or Nativity, was the most important element of every Italian home at Christmas. The *presepi* at the palazzo was over a hundred years old, had been hand-carved in Naples, and the gorgeous figurines had filled her with wonder every year.

"What if we do a few festive things together? Just because your father doesn't enjoy the holiday as much as he once did, doesn't mean you can't." She was silent a moment, then added, "Maybe we just have to remind him how beautiful Christmas really is."

"He won't like it," Rocca answered quickly. "We tried once to decorate a little tree in the nursery at the palazzo and he threw it away."

"Well, he can't throw away something that I buy, not if it's mine," Monet answered.

"Papà will make you."

"No, he can't. He won't. I might work for him, but he doesn't own me."

The children gave her a pitying look, which didn't sit well with her at all, and not only because she wasn't the least bit afraid of their father, but also because they didn't realize that it was the Uberto family that had taught her how magical Christmas could be. And it would be magical for these children, even if she had to give them the magic in little bites.

"I understand your concerns," Monet said cheerfully, "but what about me? What about *my* holiday? I can't be expected to go through Christmas without fun, can I? In London everything is so festive and beautiful right now. There are gorgeous lights and decorations everywhere, and all the stores and restaurants have dressed up their windows. Even the store I worked in had Christmas trees and decorations on every floor. My department was silver and white, with a huge silver Christmas tree with thousands of white lights just across from my desk."

"But that was London," Matteo said regretfully. "And this is Italy."

"And Italians love Christmas. Sicilians love Christmas."

"But not Papà, and we really think you'd better ask our father." Matteo glanced at his siblings and gave them a sad look, before looking back at her. "He *hates* surprises."

"I will, because *I* hate being disappointed."

Marcu made it on time for dinner and Monet really wished she could have been excused to let Marcu and his children eat together without her, but Marcu seemed to think a nanny's presence was necessary for everything.

She did make a point of saying little during the meal so the conversation could be between the children and their father, but Marcu didn't ask them very many questions and the children volunteered very little information and conversation petered out before it really began.

It was a relief when they were dismissed for bed but then Marcu stopped her as she rose, saying he expected to see her after she'd finished putting the children to bed.

She nodded that she'd heard and then continued ushering the children out, even as she processed the fact that he never hugged them or kissed them, or said anything loving and tender when saying good-night. You'd almost think he was running some form of military school. It hurt her heart, not just for the children's sake, but for his as well.

A half hour later she came back downstairs and joined Marcu in the smaller living room, having already learned that this was the room he favored in the evenings because the wooden shutters could be closed against the cold glass, keeping out the chill, and a fire could be laid in the stone hearth, making the room warm and cozy.

The ceiling was vaulted and lined with dark beams, and the fabric on the chairs and sofa was a lovely burnt pumpkin brocade, with vivid blue tiled end tables with a matching cobalt-blue wash on the inside of the huge hearth. One wall was lined with glass book cabinets, while another wall featured vivid modern art in pinks, oranges and blues. The room, centuries old, exuded elegance and money and style. No one knew how to layer fabrics and use color like the Italians.

"I'm concerned about the children," she said abruptly, taking the same chair she'd sat in last night.

"What was that?" he asked, glancing up from the book he was reading. It was the same book that had been on the table last night, and she'd glimpsed the title, something to do with politics, economics and world currencies. She couldn't imagine reading a huge book on such a subject matter but then, she wasn't an investment banker or venture capitalist, either.

"Your children shocked me today."

He closed the book. "How so?"

"They told me they don't celebrate Christmas, and I didn't believe them, telling them Christmas was always a special time at the palazzo in Palermo—"

"That was before," he interrupted, placing his book on the table at his elbow. "We don't make a fuss about Christmas anymore. It's not appropriate in light of things."

Monet decided to feign ignorance. "What things? Has the church stopped celebrating the birth of Christ?"

"No, of course not."

"They why would you not celebrate Christmas with your children?"

"We go to Mass."

"And?"

"And what?" he retorted impatiently.

"Where is the Nativity scene? Rocca and Antonio are the perfect age to enjoy the *presepi*, and you always had such a beautiful one in Palermo. In fact, there were three at one time, each set up in a different room of the palazzo."

"But we're not in Palermo," he said.

"You couldn't bring one with you? Or buy one for your children to enjoy here?"

"We're here for just three or four weeks, it seems silly to drag something like that all the way here."

She studied him a long moment. "Is that also why there are no Christmas decorations? No tree? No pretty lights or greenery around the doors, or windows? I understand you dragged skis and skates here, but nothing to celebrate the season?"

He stirred uncomfortably. "We don't make a fuss over Christmas."

"Why? Christmas was a gorgeous, special time in your family."

"That was before," he retorted curtly, rising from his chair to go stoke the fire. "Things have changed. We have different traditions now."

"But to eliminate the wonder of Christmas for your children? There are so many lovely, festive things you could do and enjoy as a family—"

"I've chosen not to."

"They miss it, though."

He added a log to the fire before turning to face her. "How can they miss what they don't know?" he demanded. "They can't."

"Matteo remembers. He was telling me about how Christmas used to be. The younger ones were all ears. They'd love to experience some of the fun and traditions that other children their age enjoy."

"No." He clasped his hands behind his back and stood tall and resolute. "It's not something we do in our family. Not anymore."

She looked at him steadily, her gaze meeting his and holding. "Well, I do. Christmas is important to me and I'm not going to give it up for you. That's not part of our deal, so I'm going to make the most of the next few weeks and have my tree, and decorate it, and go listen to carols, and do my holiday baking and anything else that makes this season so special to me."

"You can do what you want in your time, but you're not to include the children."

She couldn't help her gurgle of laughter. Was he serious? And just what time was her time?

Her laughter made his expression darker,

grimmer. His jaw jutted and his mouth tightened and he truly seemed to believe he could
give her orders and have them obeyed.

Not happening.

"Marcu, you're not thinking this through,"
she said more gently. "You've brought me here
to take care of the children. There is no backup
nanny. I don't have time 'off.' I don't have areas
that are only mine—"

"You have your own suite of rooms. You can
do what you want in there, but not in the nursery, or their individual bedrooms."

"So I can decorate my suite?"

"It's your own room." He hesitated. "But you
can't bring the children into your room, and
they can't know about your decorations—"

"Stop. Listen to yourself. You're being ridiculous, you are. When did you become such an
ogre, Marcu?"

"I don't like Christmas," he said sharply, "and
I'm not going to have you confusing the children. We enjoy this month, we do, but we enjoy
it the way I think is best, which is with little
fanfare and drama."

"So there is no Christmas miracle for you?"

He gave her an almost savage look, blue eyes

glittering beneath black brows. "There is certainly no miracle."

"You've lost your faith."

He picked up the poker and jabbed the logs furiously, sending sparks shooting up into the chimney. "You know nothing about it, and you'd be wise to drop the whole subject now."

The words were as sharp and hot as the sparks, and Monet let them swirl around her a moment before she answered. "I think I understand a little bit," she said quietly before drawing a quick breath for courage. "This is about Galeta. You lost her before Christmas."

"I didn't *lose* her. We were not careless with her. She wasn't misplaced, or lost. She was at home, with her family, with her newborn. She was where she belonged." His hard voice cracked. "And then God took her."

Monet drew another breath. "God didn't take her. Galeta was mortal. Her body failed her—"

"Che palle!"

The oath was mild but his expression was pained.

"To take a young mother from her three children," he gritted, tossing aside the poker. "Children who were just babies. A newborn just days old. My wife had a family that needed her, and loved her, and I don't know how to do this without her. I can't do this without her. So don't talk to me about faith, because you'd question yours, too, should you lose someone so fundamental to your life."

And then he walked out.

Marcu was gone in the morning when Monet woke up, leaving a note for her that he expected her to follow his instructions and if she wasn't clear on his expectations, all she had to do was call, and he'd scribbled his phone number.

After dressing, Monet headed to the nursery to oversee breakfast. As the children ate, they discussed their day.

"I was thinking we could talk to Cook and see if she'd let us visit the kitchen later and make some Christmas cookies. I don't know if you have a favorite kind but I remember the delicious *cuccidati* we used to have at the palazzo, filled with figs, dates, walnuts, spices and a hint of orange."

Elise, the housemaid, had just entered the room to collect the morning dishes and smiled as she heard mention of the Sicilian cookies.

"*Cuccidati* are a lot of work, and I'm not sure Cook has all the ingredients right now, but I am certain you could make *canestrelli* or even *pizzicati* without too much effort. Would you like me to ask Cook?"

The children answered with a resounding yes and then after Elise had gone, Monet helped Antonio dress. Matteo and Rocca didn't need or want help from her. Once hair was brushed, and teeth were clean, they resumed discussion about what to do after they were done with cookies—if Cook would allow them into the kitchen.

"Any ideas?" Monet asked them, buoyed by their eager faces. "Suggestions?"

"What could we do?" Matteo asked.

"Well, I suggest we go to the Christmas market in the village tonight," Monet said. "We'll go have dinner there and shop and see if we can't find some pretty ornaments and trinkets to decorate our own Christmas tree."

"But we don't even have a Christmas tree," Rocca reminded Monet.

"Then that is the first thing we'll do today. We'll go find a tree, and have someone help us cut it down and bring it in to the nursery."

Matteo looked skeptical. "I don't think this is a good idea. Father won't like it."

"We're not putting it in his bedroom. Or his study. Or his living room. It's going in your room." Monet studied their suddenly pinched, anxious faces. They really were nervous and that wasn't her intention. "Or," she added thoughtfully, "we could just put it in my room. I would love a Christmas tree. It'd make my room so cozy at night and it'd make it smell wonderful during the day."

"But then when we will see it?" Antonio asked. "I want a Christmas tree. I want a tree with pretty lights and ornaments and things."

She drew Antonio onto her lap. "You can always come into my room. In fact, we can have evening stories and prayers in my room. It will be quite festive. Cookies and stories every night before bed." Monet glanced from one face to the next. "How does that sound?"

"So nice…" Rocca said with a wistful sigh.

But Matteo looked troubled. "I still don't think Papà will like it. He'll say we're being sneaky."

"Then let's not do it," Monet said. "The last thing I want you to do is get in trouble. This is supposed to be a fun time of year, not a time for you to be troubled or anxious."

For a moment no one said anything and then Antonio whispered, "So you're not going to have a tree, Signorina Wilde?"

"I'd like one," she answered truthfully. "Even if it's just a very small tree. I could put it on the desk."

"Or on that table by your couch," Rocca said. "That way you could see it from your bed, too."

Monet smiled. "That is a good idea. I'd like that."

"Can we help decorate it?" Rocca asked.

"I want to, I want to," Antonio cried. "Please can I help?"

"And help pick it out? We could all go look for it together." Rocca looked hopeful. "We could even help cut it and carry it—"

"No, I think we'll leave the cutting to someone else," Monet interrupted with a smile. "But I don't see why you couldn't give me some advice. I can always use advice."

"And then we will put it in your room. There's no reason we can't go there just at night and say good-night to the tree. It's not being that sneaky. We're just saying a quick good-night, and that shouldn't make Papà too mad at us." She darted a swift glance at Matteo, and then at Monet. "He'd just be mad at Monet."

"But we don't want Papà mad at Monet," Matteo said irritably. "It's not fair for her to get in trouble for something we want."

"That's true. If we really want a tree, then we should just tell him so," Rocca said. "And if he shouts, he shouts."

Matteo shook his head. "Papà doesn't shout. He just frowns a lot and gets that expression that makes you think he's never going to smile again."

"I've seen that expression," Monet said. "It wasn't always that way, though. He used to smile a great deal. When he was younger, when I knew him before, he smiled all the time."

"He smiled before Mamma died," Matteo said quietly. "I remember our last Christmas here, before Antonio was born." He looked at his sister. "Do you remember? It was the best Christmas. It was so happy. Like a fairy tale."

The children fell silent. Monet's chest suddenly ached and her eyes felt hot and gritty.

It was the best Christmas.
Like a fairy tale.

Their innocent words pricked her heart and made her want to wrap her arms around them and keep them safe.

What a hard time they'd had of it. How impossible to lose their mother, and their father, because they had lost Marcu, too. He'd lost all joy, and love, and tenderness. It was a tragedy on top of tragedy. She exhaled slowly, letting out some of the bottled air, and said quietly, "It can be that way again. It will be that way again, one day, I promise."

"How?" Rocca asked.

Monet reached out to stroke the girl's dark silky hair, and Rocca leaned into the caress and Monet gave her head another comforting touch. "Maybe it's time we started reminding him of just how beautiful and special Christmas really is."

It was an extremely busy day, packed with activities from baking cookies to sampling cookies, to dressing in winter gear to tramp through the snow-dusted garden in search of a tree somewhere on the grounds that would be the perfect tree. It took them nearly an hour before they found one they could all agree on, and then they went in search of a gardener to cut it down and bring it inside for them.

There was much discussion about where the tree should go in Monet's room, and they moved it from spot to spot, all while Antonio begged to let them put it in the nursery. But Matteo was adamant that his father would be livid if he found it there and Monet agreed with Matteo. "We don't want your father livid," Monet said.

Once they had the tree positioned in its metal stand, they discussed how they should decorate it. The children made paper snowflakes and colored some stars, and just before they hung them on the tree, the butler appeared with a box of Christmas decorations he'd found in the attic. The children carefully went through the box, oohing and aahing at the old, and very fragile glass ornaments, and the wooden hand-carved ornaments depicting angels and wise men and shepherds and animals from the manger. They were still looking through all the ornaments, deciding which ones were small enough and light enough, to go on their little tree, when the butler returned with a long string of white lights.

The children abandoned the ornaments to help her wind the lights through the tree branches and then hang the ornaments they'd selected from the box, along with the white snowflakes they'd made. They were delighted with their finished product and begged to eat their dinner in front of the fire in her room so they could enjoy the tree. Cook made them a special meal of pizza and they all sat around on her living-room floor with their pizza and their homemade cookies, proud of everything they had accomplished today.

Monet smiled as the children chattered, telling herself everything was fine, but secretly, she had knots in her stomach, and her stomach cramped with anxiety.

Marcu wasn't going to be happy when he returned.

Marcu would probably be livid.

This was exactly the kind of day he wouldn't approve of, and yet the children were beyond thrilled. As they prepared for bed, they were positively giddy, reliving the day, and how they'd found the tree and picked ornaments from the box.

But fortunately, he wouldn't be home just yet. Fortunately they had another full day before he returned late tomorrow afternoon, or tomorrow night.

CHAPTER SEVEN

THE WINTER STORM warnings worried Marcu, and he wrapped up his meetings early, and was in his helicopter flying north, when it became apparent it was foolish to try to land in Aosta. Snow had begun to fall and the wind was howling and the only way he'd make it to the *castello* tonight would be to drive from Milan. Fortunately, his assistant had booked a car for him, and the car was waiting at the Milan airport when the helicopter landed.

Relieved to be behind the wheel, Marcu left the city, and tried to relax as he got on the open road, but the sky was dark and ominous and the news reports indicated foul weather for the next few days, with this new storm being the worst so far this year.

As he drove, he wondered what the children had been doing, and he hoped Monet had gotten them outside for fresh air and exercise. He tried to think of the children but not Monet, which was impossible. The more he tried to block her from his thoughts, the more she consumed them.

He'd been so preoccupied with her even last night when he'd taken Vittoria to dinner. He hadn't wanted to be at dinner with Vittoria. He sat across the table from her thinking that maybe Monet was right, maybe he was making a mistake, and not because he needed a warm wife, but the children needed a warm, tender mother. Only as he listened to Vittoria discuss the ski trip, and the people who would be there, and the parties they'd been invited to, his chest tightened, the air bottling in his lungs. Not once did she ask about his children. Not once did she express concern that it might be difficult for the children to be left behind for the holiday.

What if she was as cold and hard as he was?

What if the children suffered more if he married her?

"I have to tell you something," he'd said, putting down his fork. "I kissed Monet, the woman who is staying with the children while Miss Sheldon is gone. It shouldn't have happened, and it won't happen again. I'm sorry—"

"If it was a one-off, and it won't happen again, why are you telling me?" she asked, coolly. "Was there a reason for me to know?"

"I feel badly about it."

She gave him a long level look before shrugging. "I have never imagined you to be a saint. You will do what you want—"

"But I don't, and I wouldn't when we marry." *If we marry*, he silently added, before wondering where that came from.

He wasn't having serious doubts, was he?

He couldn't let Monet turn everything inside out.

"Men have affairs," Vittoria answered matter-of-factly. "Women do, too. It's human nature."

"I never cheated on Galeta. If we married, I wouldn't cheat on you," he said grimly.

"If," she said, head tipping, long hair spilling over her shoulder. "You are not so sure now, are you? A few days with this nanny from your childhood, and you kiss her, and then question our relationship. Perhaps you have feelings for her."

"I did," he said, "when I was younger, before I married Galeta."

"Perhaps you still do now."

Dinner ended soon after that, and he drove Vittoria back to her apartment, and he left her after seeing her to her door.

Back in his car he'd felt wildly out of sorts. Kissing Monet had changed everything. It shouldn't have because the kiss was brief. It had lasted less than a minute. There had been no touching, no exploration of skin or curves… and yet he might as well have stripped her bare because her body was so imprinted on his mind and imagination.

He'd felt her soft breasts against his chest. He'd felt the shape of her hips, and the indentation of her waist. He'd felt the heat of her slim body and the vanilla-and-orange-blossom scent of her hair and skin.

She'd smelled like summer and her fragrance had stayed with him long after he'd gone to bed, making him think of home, and a past that was long gone.

On the one hand she was vastly different from the girl she'd been, and on the other, she was exactly the same girl—strong, smart, authentic, original.

He'd never met anyone like Monet. She was

so opposite him in every way and yet somehow it had once felt right.

Now...

Now...

But there was no now, he told himself tersely, tension weighting his limbs. He still needed a wife, and Vittoria had met the children and it could be a good marriage. He hadn't married Galeta because he'd loved her, but he'd respected her, and he respected Vittoria. Love was inconsequential. Security mattered. Stability mattered. He wasn't going to risk the future—or his children's mental health—on something as temporary, and unstable, as romantic love.

Not that he'd ever loved Monet, either. But there had been desire. Fierce desire. Desire that had destroyed a six-year relationship and created a serious chasm between him and his father.

He had to smash the desire now. He had to get control of himself immediately. There was no way he'd allow an impulse to wreck his plans. He knew what he wanted, and he knew what he didn't want and his decision had been made.

Exhaling, Marcu turned the windshield wipers on higher, needing the increased speed to clear the falling snow from the windshield. The snow was coming down harder. The wind was blowing sheets of snow across the road, turning the world beyond his car a blinding white. It was going to be a long drive to the *castello* tonight.

By the time he arrived home, the children were in bed, asleep—he knew, because he checked in on them and they were all in their beds, tucked in against the night's chill. Marcu went to Monet's room and knocked on the door, wanting to see how things had gone while he'd been away.

It took her a few moments to come to the door and he wondered if she'd also gone to bed. He was just turning away when her door opened and she peeked out, her long dark hair tumbling free over her shoulders, her eyes lovely and luminous in her pale oval face.

"Did I wake you?" he asked, feeling guilty for disturbing her, and yet it wasn't that late, not even quite nine.

"No, I was just in bed reading."

"How was everything here? I didn't hear from you so I hope things went smoothly."

"Very smoothly," she answered. "We get along very well. So well, that the time just flies by."

There was something in her cheerful answer that sounded a little forced. "What did you do to pass the time?" he asked.

"We made cookies, and played in the snow." She smiled brightly up at him, still holding the door close so that all he could see of her was her head and part of her shoulder. "We had lots of fresh air. I've put your winter coats and boots to good use."

"You're making me suspicious," he said.

"Why?"

"You seem determined to be happy—"

"But I am happy," she interrupted. "I really enjoy your children. We have a lot of fun together."

And that's when he spotted a bit of sparkle behind her shoulder. It was a gleam of light, reflecting off something silver and shiny and then he took a breath and smelled fragrant pine.

Marcu reached above her head and gave the door a push, forcing it open. In her sitting room on the table near her hearth stood a shimmering tree with white lights and colorful glass ornaments. It was small but beautifully decorated and the fresh smell filled her room, making him immediately feel nostalgic.

For a moment he couldn't speak, and then he drew a slow, measured breath, fighting to remain in control. "I thought we agreed there would be no decorations, no tree, none of this nonsense—"

"I didn't agree," she interrupted hotly, arms crossing over her chest. "*I* never agreed, because I completely disagree with you—"

"That doesn't matter. Your opinion doesn't matter. You're here to do what I tell you."

"Wrong. You're here because you trust me to take care of your children, and I am."

"I don't celebrate Christmas, Monet."

"Fine, but must you deprive the children? Are they no longer allowed to experience the beauty of it? I understand you are grieving, and they also continue to grieve, but you are turning their loss into a greater punishment. You are taking the loss of their mother and turning it into the loss of all hope and beauty—"

"Rubbish!" he snapped, silencing her again, his voice growing louder, his temper hotter. She was trying his patience and he didn't like it. Marcu stepped all the way into her room and closed the door behind him.

"You have spent too much time in England now," he added, stalking toward the hearth, which glowed with red embers. He circled the table with the tree, feeling emotions he didn't welcome. "You have bought in to this very commercialized idea of Christmas," he said, looking back at her. "In Sicily, Christmas was never about trees and decorations and presents. I give my children presents on Epiphany. You will see that my children eagerly await for the arrival of Le Befana and the sweets they've hoped for. They will receive little toys and treats if they have been good, and that's our heritage, our tradition, and they don't need your British Christmas."

For a moment there was just silence and then she shook her head, making her long hair dance. "Fine. Have your way. They don't need it. You don't need it. But *I* do. I need my Christmas. You called in a favor, but that favor did not include stripping me of all the things that give my life meaning, and I want to celebrate Christmas. I want to have magic and fizz and joy. So if you don't like it, please send me away now. I would love to return to London and my friends and my life there. Let me leave right now, because I am not going to battle with you on this. I think you are wrong, I think you are actually dreadful—"

"Dreadful?" he practically roared.

"Yes, dreadful," she repeated, stepping close and jabbing a finger in the air, "and hurtful."

He took a step back, affronted. "I am neither."

"Yes, you are, and you enjoy being a beast, too. Now I realize you were left with three children and a broken heart, but face life, and face the pain and let your heart heal. Let your children's hearts heal. Move forward without this anger, because right now I feel sorry for Vittoria. I pity any woman you want to bring into this family because you are not ready. You are not ready for a new wife, and you are not ready to let go of the past."

"The children—"

"This isn't about the children! This is about *you*. This is about you being angry at God, and angry with yourself, because you are not God and you couldn't be there and you couldn't save

Galeta. Heavens, you have serious issues and you need to deal with them."

Rage swept through him. His hands balled at his sides. "How dare you talk to me this way?"

She threw her head back, her eyes flashing fire, not in the least bit intimidated by his roar. "How dare others *not* talk to you this way? They do you no favors. They're hurting you by keeping the truth from you."

"I've had enough. In the morning you will remove the tree—"

"No. That will not happen."

"If you don't dispose of it, I will."

"If you touch my tree, I am gone. And if you choose to fire me, that's fine, too, because I never wanted to be in your employ in the first place. I came here to do you a favor, and whether you like it or not, I am your equal in every way."

"You're being paid. That makes you my employee."

"Keep your awful money. I don't want it. I never wanted it. The only thing I ever wanted from you was respect, and it was the one thing you have refused to give me."

"You're hysterical!"

"Not hysterical, just honest. I'm done holding back. I'm done worrying about your ego. You have far too much ego. Marcu, you are a man, not a god, or a demigod. You are a human being, and because you're human you make mistakes, and you are making mistakes right now, and that would be okay if you could recognize it and work on it but you won't."

"Are you finished?" he gritted.

"No. I'm not going to tiptoe around you, and I'm not going to pretend that you are right, when you're not. I'm not afraid of you, and I don't care what you think of me. It's not as if I'm going to lose your good opinion. Marcu, I know what you think of me. I know exactly what you and your father have always thought of me. It's why I left Palermo. It's why I left all of you. I wasn't good enough. I wasn't *worthy*."

The words came faster and faster and he sensed she'd been keeping them bottled up for years, and now she could no longer hold them back.

"I know that I was kind of woman you'd take to your bed," she added, "but you'd never respect enough to marry. I was the kind of woman who'd fulfil your physical desires but never win your heart—"

"You're talking nonsense now," he snapped, his own patience tested, his own control threatened.

"*No.* I heard you. I heard you and your father the night he found us in your bedroom. I heard what he said when he pulled you out into the hallway. He asked if you were being careful, and if you'd used protection, because you couldn't be stupid and fall for my schemes as I was not the kind of woman you'd ever marry." Monet's voice quavered and she reached up to press a trembling hand to her forehead. After a moment she continued. "I heard every word he said, just as I'm sure he intended me to. He wanted me to know that I was not the kind of woman you could take out socially. He wanted me to hear that I was a whore like my mother—"

"He did *not* use the word *whore*," Marcu interrupted gruffly, stunned that she'd heard the conversation in the hall all those years ago. He hadn't known she'd heard what his father had said, hadn't realized that his father's voice had carried so clearly. No wonder she was so hurt and angry. She'd bottled up the pain for years and now it was spilling out of her in a torrent of words.

"You're right. He used a different word, a Sicilian swear word that implied almost the same thing, but what it boils down to is that I wasn't acceptable due to being a bastard."

"My father wasn't trying to hurt you, he was trying to protect me as I was the oldest, and his heir."

"He was your father. He was doing what he thought was best," she said, lips curving up, contradicting the bright sheen of tears in her eyes. "I guess it was a blessing in disguise. It proved beneficial to hear his thoughts—and yours—clarifying many things for me, and allowing me to make a break from you."

"He hurt you, and I'm sorry."

"*You* hurt me, and you're not sorry." Her chin jerked up and tears clung to her lower lashes. "But in hindsight, I'm glad you didn't defend me. It was important to hear that conversation and discover you had no feelings for me. It was a giant wake-up call, one that I desperately needed as it was time for me to stop living my life to please the Ubertos. That conversation freed me, which is why I can stand here and look at you and not feel inferior."

Marcu didn't know what to do with her. He didn't know how to stop these words because they were barbed and brutal and coming at him so fast. Is this why she'd left first thing in the morning? Is this truly the reason she'd fled the palazzo?

"You should have told me you'd heard him," he said tautly. "You should have confronted me—"

"And what would you have done? Denied it? Told me I'd misheard? That I didn't understand? Marcu, I understood perfectly then, and I understand now, but none of that matters. What matters is the family here, in this *castello*. It's time for you to deal with your grief so you can take care of your children. *You* need to love them. You need to love them so well that you don't need a woman to come in and fix things for you. Because you don't need a wife. You don't need a new mother for them. You just need to forgive yourself for not being there when Galeta died. And you could be an amazing father if you stopped looking back and just focused on the present. Your children are adorable. They're smart and kind and funny. They are perfect. And they are still *so* young. All they need is someone to love them and laugh with them. Why can't that be you?"

Her words were relentless, sharp and heavy, and they were piercing the armor he wore to keep from feeling too much. "I think you've said enough for one night," he growled.

"Then leave. This is my room. You're free to go at any time."

"You're trying to provoke me."

"You're refusing to see what's in front of your face!"

He stalked toward her. "You, you mean?"

Every time he took a step forward, she took a step back. "No, your children," she snapped.

She was skirting the furniture now, and moving closer to the wall, but he wasn't about to let her escape. "You're making this about the children, but it's not," he answered. "You're angry with me, angry that I didn't defend you to my father that night—"

"I was angry then, and hurt, but that's behind us. I'm here trying to help you now. It's what you wanted. It's why you insisted I come."

"To follow my instructions," he said, finally

cornering her. There was nowhere for her to run and she stood facing him, her back to the plaster wall, her expression mutinous. "Not challenge me at every turn."

"That's because you've become lazy, and soft—"

"Soft?" he repeated incredulously.

Her golden-brown eyes flashed at him, her lips twisting scornfully. "Yes, soft. You don't want to do the hard work. You want an easy fix, but you're going to be disappointed. You're going to regret this down the road."

"I'm already regretting having you here."

"Send me home in the morning then. We'll both be happier."

She was tiny, barely reaching his shoulder, and she practically vibrated with fury and emotion and he, who avoided emotion, felt drawn to her light and heat just as a moth was drawn to a flame.

He wanted to touch her…kiss her…possess her…and yet he'd promised her he wouldn't. He'd promised her that as long as he was pursuing another woman, he wouldn't touch her, and he was determined to keep that vow. But that didn't stop him from moving closer, and leaning in, his hands against the wall over her head, and his body angling over hers. There was space between them. A sliver of space. Just enough to honor his promise, but not enough to give either of them peace of mind.

There was no peace of mind with her here.

There was no peace of mind since she'd left him all those years ago.

"You promised you wouldn't touch me," she said breathlessly.

He heard the catch in her voice, as well as the quick rise and fall of her breasts. She wasn't immune to him. No, she was just as aware of him as he was of her.

"Not going to touch you," he said, dropping his head a quarter inch, her mouth so close now that he could feel the heat shimmering between them. The heat was intoxicating. *She* was intoxicating. He felt almost drugged. "Just standing here."

Monet swallowed hard. He could see her smooth column of a throat work, and the muscle in her jaw tighten. Her eyes glowed, flecks of gold against a darker amber. Her lips were full and soft and far too tempting.

To kiss her properly, to kiss her thoroughly…

"I know what you want to do," she said, her voice pitched low, the tone so husky he thought immediately of sex and sin.

He craved sex and sin.

He craved the forbidden.

"So do I, but I haven't, have I?" he answered, a carnal rasp in his voice as he bent his elbows, lowering his body, dropping his head so that his mouth hovered over hers, feeling the warmth of her breath on his lips, and smelling the scent of her shampoo and skin. This was torture. There was no other word for it. He stared at her mouth and the soft lushness of her lower lip, fascinated by the shape. It was decadent and sensual and he wanted to claim it…and her.

His body felt taut and hard, his senses flooded with her scent and heat. Why was she the only one who made him feel this way? Why did she drive him mad? It made no sense. This desire wasn't logical and yet it was the most compelling thing he'd felt in years.

Her cheeks already flushed, darkened to a luscious rose. She chewed on her lower lip. "You're not abiding by the rules," she whispered.

"What rules?"

She closed her eyes, and drew a slow, unsteady breath before exhaling just as slowly. "Exactly my point."

Marcu's body was so hard he ached. He pressed his knuckles to the wall. He craved her mouth. He craved her taste. It was all he could do to just hold his position. "This isn't working, is it?" he muttered.

She gave her head a very slight shake.

"What do we do?" he asked.

She dragged in another unsteady breath. "One of us needs to leave."

"Leave? Your room?"

"No. This place. The *castello*." She opened her eyes, and looked straight into his. The gold-brown of her eyes was dark with emotion. She looked as if she was in pain, and it sent a lance of white-hot agony through him.

He flinched and ground his knuckles against the wall.

"We can't both be here," she whispered. "Nothing good will come of it. You know it."

He did know it, and he hated what she was saying, but she was right. This wasn't good for either of them. This was beyond torturous. He hated feeling so much. He hated feeling help-less. But to leave her…

To lose her…

Again.

And yet she wasn't his. She'd never be his. Why couldn't he accept it?

But no, he could. He did. He was an adult, a man who understood responsibility. He under-stood ramifications.

"You need to be here. I don't," he said brusquely, before peeling himself away from her and taking a step back. The effort had drained him. He felt almost beaten as he put space between them. "I'm leaving tomorrow."

"Good, because if you don't, I will."

Monet sagged as Marcu left her suite. Her heart was still racing so fast that she could barely cross to the chair by the fire before she col-lapsed into it.

She'd never wanted a kiss so badly.

She'd never wanted anything as much as she'd wanted him to throw caution to the wind and just kiss her…

And not a sweet, tentative kiss, but mad pas-sion. Her hands itched for his, her body trembled with longing. If only he'd clasped her hands and pinned them over her head and held her there against that wall as he claimed her mouth, and then claimed her.

She'd wanted the weight of his body, and the heat and pressure. Her body felt so unbearably sensitive. Monet wrapped an arm over her chest, pressing against her breasts, against the tingling in her nipples.

She'd wanted his hands there, and she'd wanted his mouth on her skin, and she'd wanted him…

My God.

This was everything she'd felt in Palermo, and yet more, because she was older now and more confident and she didn't want him because she had some big emotional hole inside of her, but rather she wanted him because he set her body on fire and torched her senses and she loved it.

Loved it.

And she wanted more.

Monet's head fell back against the back of the chair and she sighed heavily. Obviously she wouldn't be kissing Marcu, or taking him to her bed, but the desire burned within her and it wasn't going to be easy to forget just how hungry and fierce he'd made her feel.

Marcu stood at his bedroom window watching the snow fall in white sheets beyond the thick beveled glass. It was after midnight and he hadn't even tried to go to bed, knowing it would be impossible to sleep when his brain still raced, struggling to process everything said tonight.

All these years he'd thought Monet had left Palermo because she'd been disgusted by the kiss. He'd thought she'd wanted to escape, because she was filled with regret over what they'd done. He'd agonized over his actions, thinking he'd let her down, betrayed her trust. Had she viewed him as a surrogate brother, someone who would look after her instead? If that was the case, no wonder she'd given him a look of repulsion when he'd returned to his room after speaking to his father.

He'd misread the situation and violated her trust.

For years he couldn't even think of her without self-hatred, disgusted with himself for taking advantage of her and making her feel unsafe in her own home.

But she hadn't said any of that tonight. No, she'd flung different words at him instead…an altogether different accusation.

She'd been hurt by his father's words, and devastated that Marcu hadn't defended her.

He hadn't known she could hear the conversation—a conversation he remembered quite differently.

His brow creased as he stared out at the swirling world of white.

Either way, it was problematic being under the same roof with her again. He wasn't sure how he had thought this would play out. Had he imagined that he wouldn't be attracted to her any longer? Had he hoped that by bringing her to Aosta, he would finally feel free of the past? Of her?

Except that he wasn't free of the past, or her. Being near her now was even more difficult than before.

Being near her made him feel, and a dark dangerous hunger seemed to fill his veins and heat his skin. He wanted her. He wanted to possess her…to touch her and taste her, to take her, and know her, and make her shudder and come apart for him.

And yet despite the desire, and despite his body being hard and his pulse thudding with demanding need, he had a ring for Vittoria in his travel bag. He had a suitcase packed for his departure tomorrow. His head told him that Vittoria would be the right one. His head said he needed someone suitable, someone who didn't threaten his calm, and control. He preferred a rational world, a world of order and reason. Not passion. Or hunger. Or volatile emotions that weren't to be trusted.

Now if only his body would listen, and his pulse would slow, and his uncomfortable aching erection would ease.

He put a hand to the cold glass, pressing his palm against the chill, trying to freeze the heat within him.

Monet wasn't for him. She was never meant to be his. But at the same time, there was no one he trusted more with his children. They'd be safe with her.

There was no one he wanted more…

But marriage wasn't about passion, or desire. Marriage was duty, responsibility. He couldn't confuse the two.

He'd leave first thing tomorrow. He'd leave

before he did something rash, something il-logical…something that might change all their lives forever.

The snow was falling thickly in the morning when Monet dragged herself from bed. Her head ached and her eyes felt dry and gritty. She'd tossed and turned all night, her dreams tormenting her almost as much as Marcu had tormented her with the promise of something he had no intention of delivering. He'd been pretty ruthless last night, and she'd been aroused by it, wanting him more than ever.

Monet wrapped herself in her thick robe and went to the sitting room, where a breakfast tray waited on one of the small tables. Even better, there was no note from Marcu.

She plugged in the lights on her little tree and sipped her *caffe latte*, and tore apart the warm fragrant roll, liberally spreading butter and jam on it. She'd forgotten how much she loved *prima colazione*. Even though she was in the Italian Alps, not Sicily, a part of her felt as if she'd come home.

She was just finishing the last of her break-fast when a knock sounded on her door. She closed her eyes, said a swift prayer—*please don't let it be Marcu*—and then rose to open the door.

It was Marcu, dressed, in winter travel clothes.

"I've said goodbye to the children," he said flatly. "They're just waking, but I didn't want to leave without speaking to them."

"It's early," she said, thinking that just moments ago she wanted him gone and now that he was leaving, she felt strangely deflated.

"If I have any hope of getting out of the valley, it's now. It's only going to get worse later."

"You're not trying to fly, are you?"

"No. The helicopter can't land in these conditions. I'm driving. Once I reach Milan, I'll be able to fly."

She glanced out the window and couldn't even see the massive pine trees for the thickly falling snow. "How will you be able to see? And won't the roads be icy?"

"The roads won't be icy yet. I agree it's not ideal driving conditions, no. But if I don't go now, I'm here all weekend. The storm is supposed to continue for the next couple of days."

"Be safe then."

"I will." He hesitated. "There is something I

need to say before I go. Something that I should have said years ago." He hesitated again. "I helped you leave Palermo all those years ago because I thought you were…disgusted…by my attentions. I thought I had taken advantage of you, and—" he broke off and sucked in a breath "—forced myself on you. I thought that was why you were in tears when I returned to the bedroom after speaking with my father." He dropped his head and stared at the floor. "I have hated myself for hurting you. I have always wanted to make amends. It's why I came to see you after Galeta died. I thought perhaps God was cursing me—"

"No."

He made a soft, rough sound under his breath. "I am sorry if I—"

"You didn't." She rushed toward him, hand outstretched to stop his words. She was just about to put her hand to his chest when she remembered herself, and curled her fingers into a ball instead. "God wasn't cursing you, or punishing you. Nor did you take advantage of me. You did nothing improper, nothing that I didn't want. I was upset that night, but for different reasons, reasons that had to do with my eighteen-year-old heart." She struggled to smile. "I had a massive crush on you. I'd had a crush on you forever and my feelings were hurt that you didn't feel the same way about me—"

"Obviously I had feelings for you. I wouldn't have kissed you otherwise."

"Yes, but I wasn't the one you could keep, remember, and while I understand that now, it was…bruising…back then."

"I wish I'd understood better."

"It's fine. I was eighteen, and a romantic. I took the kiss too seriously, imagining possibilities that weren't there. I was wrong, and I survived." She took a step back and did a little bow. "Look! I'm here. I'm fine."

His head lifted and his gaze locked with hers. "One last thing, before I go."

She swallowed hard and forced a smile. "You're making it sound like this is the last time I'll see you. You're not intending on driving recklessly, are you?"

"Of course not. I have three children who need me."

"Exactly right," she retorted. "Don't ever forget it."

"I don't." He reached up to run his hand over

his mouth, and jaw. "The favor I demanded of you. It wasn't fair of me, seeing as I put you in that position in the first place."

Monet flashed to Marcu's bedroom suite and how she'd been virtually naked in his bed, her shirt off, her bra off, just her panties on when Marcu's father had barged in. Marcu had covered her so his father hadn't seen her, but it had been obvious that Monet had little on. "It is what it is, Marcu. No one grows up without getting a little emotionally banged up."

"You were so angry with me," Marcu said quietly. "You told me you never wanted to see me again."

She nodded, remembering. "Yes."

"You meant it, too."

"I did." Her shoulders twisted. "I needed a change. And I needed to figure out my life without the Ubertos in it."

He turned to the window and looked out at the fat thick snowflakes falling steadily, relentlessly. "That's why I made you promise me that you'd return the favor one day. I was worried you were cutting me off, and I wasn't ready to lose you entirely. It was my way of letting you go, but not letting you go. The favor was my last tie to you. It represented one more conversation, one more visit, one last bit of connection."

His words put a pang in her chest and she sucked in her lower lip, biting on it, to keep from making a sound.

He'd always known how to get to her.

He'd always known the right words to say… at least until she'd left and he'd married and become someone else, someone she didn't like and didn't want to know. But it seemed that the old Marcu was still in there. The Marcu she adored wasn't entirely gone.

"I'm glad," she said simply. "It would have been tragic for us to go the rest of our lives without speaking again. I'm glad I was able to help you with your children. They are such lovely little people. You are lucky to have them."

The ache in her chest expanded, pressing into her throat, making it hard to talk and swallow. Life had a funny way of turning on itself, upending everything.

Last night she'd gone to bed, body on fire. This morning her heart felt as if it had broken free of her chest and was flopping around at her feet on the floor.

He nodded once. "I need to go."

"Yes, you do." She shot a glance out the window. "It doesn't look good, though. I'm concerned about the drive."

"Once I make it over the pass, I'll be fine."

"You mean, *if* you make it over the pass."

Marcu suddenly smiled, one of the careless, self-deprecating smiles she knew from years past, a smile she'd thought she might never see again. "You have so little faith in me."

"Not so, but with all that you have here, dependent on you, I don't know why you'd want to tempt fate."

He gave her a long look, his smile fading. "You might think I'm not listening, but I am. I have heard every word you've said."

Her chest seized, burning. She blinked hard to keep her eyes from filling with tears. "We will miss you," she said quietly. "Be careful."

"Always," he answered, after a moment's silence, before turning and walking out.

CHAPTER EIGHT

MONET AND THE children spent the morning playing card games and then helping the cook make pasta in the huge stone kitchen that had managed to marry medieval and modern.

The cook was showing the children how to gently fold the pasta and pinch the seams when the butler stepped into the kitchen and gestured for Monet to follow him.

"I just received a call from the police," the butler said quietly. "*Signor*'s car was found. It went over the embankment—"

"Over the embankment?" Monet interrupted, heart faltering. "What do you mean?"

The butler frowned, as if not sure how to make it more clear. "Off the road, over the edge."

Suddenly her grasp of Italian seemed inadequate. "Off the road, over the edge…of the mountain?"

"He wasn't in the car. They don't know where

he is. But he wouldn't be able to walk away if he wasn't okay," the butler reasoned.

Or, he was injured and concussed and wandered away from his car to freeze to death in some ravine. Monet swallowed hard. "Was there blood in the car? Had the air bag deployed?"

"The police didn't say. They are looking for him now."

She walked to the tall window overlooking the summer herb garden, a garden currently buried by three feet of snow. All you could see in the walled garden was white—white everywhere—and the snow just kept falling.

Where was Marcu?

Was he hurt? Or had he been plucked from the road and was right now traveling to Milan, courtesy of some kind stranger?

But if that was the case, wouldn't he call? Send word?

She chewed on a knuckle, heartsick. He shouldn't have gone. It was foolish…dangerous… Stupid man.

Rocca pushed the kitchen door open and peeked around the corner. "Signorina Wilde, you're missing all the fun!"

Monet forced a smile. "I'll be right there. Give me just a minute."

The door closed and Monet turned to the butler. "How will the police track him in the snow? I'd think the snow would be covering up his footsteps."

"I don't know."

She held her breath, scared for Marcu, scared for the children. "Do you have the phone number for someone leading the investigation?"

"No, I don't, and I'm not certain it's reached the investigation stage yet."

"Even though Marcu Uberto's car has been found down in an embankment and he's not in it?"

"We're in a very rural area. This isn't the city."

Monet bit her lip and looked over her shoulder to the kitchen door, thinking of the children inside making pasta. This was the last thing they needed.

The butler must have read her thoughts as he asked, "I wasn't sure if you wanted to say anything to the children."

Monet was at least adamant about this and

gave her head a firm shake. "No. Not until we know something conclusive."

Monet was reading stories to the children when a snowplow could be heard outside, scraping the road leading to the *castello*.

She went to the window to watch the huge plow clearing snow. The children joined her at the window. The snowplow stopped not far from the entrance, and a door opened and the driver got out, and then the driver helped a passenger out.

"Papà!" Antonio cried, tapping the glass.

Monet watched as the snowplow driver aided Marcu to the front door. Staff were now spilling out of the house, rushing down the stairs to help.

"I'll be right back," she told the children before racing downstairs, where Marcu was now in the entrance hall.

He looked soaked through, but he was home. The staff continued to swarm him, and Monet pressed forward as well until she remembered her place—she wasn't his girlfriend, wasn't a friend, wasn't family, and wasn't even really staff—and she fell back a step, allowing others to see to him. But even then, her gaze swept over him, intently studying him from head to toe.

He had abrasions on his face, a cut on the bridge of his nose, and another on his cheekbone, plus the makings of a fine bruise on his brow.

He was standing, but just barely, and he gratefully accepted the help of the butler and steward as they each wrapped an arm around him, supporting him as they ushered him to the staircase, heading up to his room. The cook was given instructions to prepare a hot drink and meal, and housekeeping went to build fires in his rooms.

Marcu passed her on the staircase and his gaze met hers. His expression was one of utter weariness. "I should have listened to you," he said.

"You're safe. That's what's important," she answered.

He appeared to want to say something else and then he changed his mind and he continued up the staircase to his suite of rooms.

Monet didn't see Marcu until much later that night. After coming home, he'd showered and gone to bed and stayed there for hours. It wasn't until dinner that he emerged from his room and joined his family at the table in the dining room.

The children were subdued as they took in his cuts and bruises. He told them he'd had an accident driving, and after crashing he'd set off on foot to get help. After forty-five minutes of walking in what he feared were circles, he'd come to a rural house, and met a farmer, and the farmer attached a snowplow to the front of his tractor and slowly drove him all the way back to the *castello*.

The kids had dozens of questions, which Marcu patiently answered. Yes, the cab was small, but it was high up with pretty good visibility. The cab was also new so there was heating. Yes, they were squished but he was so grateful for the farmer's help that he didn't mind being in such cramped conditions. He also mentioned that the tractor had a snow-blower on the back, and they were using that but it had stopped working partway.

Cook had made a delicious almond cake with spiced pears and *crème anglaise* for dessert and after the children had eaten, Monet whispered that they should go give their father a hug and kiss good-night because they were lucky to have him home in one piece.

Marcu seemed caught off guard by the hugs and kisses. He returned them, a little awkwardly, but the children seemed pleased and Rocca gave her father an extra squeeze and kiss.

"You'll come back down afterward?" Marcu said to Monet as she shepherded the children out the dining-room door.

She nodded, returning almost an hour later because the children had so many questions about their father's accident and if he was still going to leave them for Christmas or if this meant he'd be with them after all.

Monet couldn't answer their questions, and encouraged them to ask him themselves tomorrow, after they'd had a good night's sleep.

"Was it hard to get them to settle tonight?" he asked as she entered the room. Marcu was lying on the sofa, his arm over his eyes.

"Does the light hurt your eyes?" she asked.

"I've a headache I can't shake," he answered.

"Can I get you something?"

"I've taken some tablets. I'm sure it will be better tomorrow."

"You probably have a concussion."

"Probably," he agreed. "It was a hard fall."

"The air bag didn't help then?"

"It did. I hit my head when I was trying to climb out of the ravine. I hit a patch of ice and went down, face-first." He dropped his arm and dragged himself up into a sitting position. "Serves me right for thinking I could handle the roads. There was no one else out there."

"You're alive, and that's what matters." Monet realized how trite that sounded and quickly added, "Well, that's what the children were saying. They said extra prayers for you tonight, grateful you were home with them."

Marcu grimaced but said nothing.

She sat down on the edge of a chair facing him. "I think you should join the children for their prayers and stories," she said. "They need you. They want you."

"I don't want to do prayers."

"Let them say their own prayers and you can read them a story." She hesitated. "The point is, they crave time with you, and the bedtime routine is an important ritual. It makes them feel safe, and they need to feel safe with you."

"They are safe with me. I will always protect them."

Monet picked her words carefully. "But part of feeling safe is being emotionally secure. It's having the children comfortable with you, and secure in the knowledge that you want to know them for who they are, not who they should be. And that happens when they can share their thoughts and feelings, and bedtime is perfect for that. It's a lovely time, an informal time, and takes just a half hour. I understand when you are out of town it makes sense for a babysitter to do this, but if you are here, you should be the one in there, hearing their thoughts and validating their feelings."

He closed his eyes and rubbed his temple on the side without the bruise. "You certainly have a lot of opinions."

"I never had my mother's attention at bedtime. By bedtime she was already with your father. I used to wish someone was there to hear my thoughts." Her voice suddenly cracked, and Monet felt mortified for saying so much. She didn't like talking about how lonely she'd been growing up. Life before she and her mother arrived at the palazzo had been chaotic, and tumultuous. It had been a relief to arrive in Palermo and stay put in one place for as long they did.

"You must have resented us," he said quietly.

She shrugged. "Not really. If I resented anyone, it was my mother. I loved your family. You gave me my first taste of family life. I told your children I never experienced a proper Christmas before I lived with your family. You had traditions and customs and I loved it."

He was silent a moment. "And then I took that all from you."

Her breath caught, and she stammered, "I would have had to leave sooner or later."

"Later would have been better for you, wouldn't it?"

She glanced down at her hands, her fingers knotting. "I wasn't going to live with my mother forever," she said before looking back at Marcu. "We'd agreed that I'd support myself once I turned eighteen, and I'd turned eighteen, so it was time."

"I wish I wasn't the reason you left, though."

She dragged in a slow breath, wondering how

they'd even ended up here, on this topic. "I thought we were discussing the children," she said huskily, "and how much they'd enjoy you tucking them in at night."

"I will do it tomorrow night," he said. He glanced at her, lips twisting. "I hope that makes you happy."

"It does, because it will make them happy."

His gaze locked with hers, the blue irises bright. "And what would make you happy, Monet Wilde?"

Monet felt heat wash through her, rising up to sweep her cheeks. "I don't know how to answer that. It's an awfully open-ended question."

"Is there nothing that would make you happy?"

"Knowing you were closer to your children would make me happy. Knowing that they come before all else—"

"They do," he interrupted, "and this isn't about them. This is about you."

She said nothing. She didn't know how to answer him, in part because she didn't know her feelings. She'd been torn ever since she'd arrived in Aosta Valley. Being near Marcu was puzzling...bewildering. She wanted him, but she couldn't have him. She wanted him to want her, and then she was terrified of his touch because she knew she couldn't resist him.

"I've ended it with Vittoria," he said abruptly, rising from the couch to pace the length of the carpet before the fire. "I told her it's not going to work, and that I'm sorry if I had misled her."

Monet opened her mouth, closed it, still unable to make a single sound.

He faced the fire as he spoke. "She said she wasn't surprised. In fact, she sounded almost…relieved. Apparently she had some serious qualms about taking on another woman's children."

"She didn't say that!"

"She did. And more." He shrugged wearily as he turned to face her. "She had worried that the children might impact our social life and all the travel she'd imagined we would do."

"I'm sorry."

"I'm not. You were right, about so many things."

"Like what?"

"Marriage has to be more than just a contract. Marriage must have some emotions, somewhere. She felt nothing for me, or the children."

"Then why be with you? Why date you?"

He laughed without humor. "I'm rich."

"And handsome."

He gave her a swift glance. "Am I?"

Monet didn't know whether to laugh or cry. "You're impossible."

"So you've been telling me."

"You've had a horrible day," she said, even as her heart galloped. It was ridiculous, still carrying this torch for him. He wasn't a beast. He was just a man who had suffered terribly.

"But it's ending the way it should. I'm here, with my family, and out of a relationship that wasn't a good one, and might have proved disastrous for my children." His lips curved faintly. "I suppose I owe you my gratitude."

"You can keep it. I don't want it."

"Why not?"

"We go back a very long way. Despite what happened at the end, you were my friend when I needed one, and I am simply trying to be a friend now, as it seems you need one."

He made a rough raw sound. "You are so much more than a friend."

Monet found herself watching him, feeling like a girl again, impossibly infatuated with someone out of her reach. Marcu intrigued her, fascinated her, spoke to her in a way that no one else did. It was easy not dating when no one appealed to you. Monet wasn't attracted to most men in her sphere. She simply wasn't interested. The idea of trying to find "someone" for her left her cold. But Marcu made her feel. Marcu made something in her warm, and quicken. She was so alive in his company. It made no sense. But then it had never made sense.

Suddenly he was focused on her again, and their eyes locked and held.

For once she didn't try to hide her raw emotions—the good, and the bad—and she stared back at him, feeling the full weight of her awareness, as well as her bewilderment that he could still impact her so.

She shouldn't still want him. She shouldn't still long for a night with him. She ached for all the things she hadn't ever known. Her body tingled, her skin prickled, her pulse drummed. He had taken so many women to his bed and yet he never taken her there. It was good, she told herself, she shouldn't be there. But on the other hand, she wasn't eighteen anymore, she was an adult. A woman. And she could make love to whomever she wanted.

And she wanted Marcu.

If she was going to belong to anyone, it should be him.

"I should go to bed," she said hoarsely. "It's late and it's been an exhausting day."

"What are your plans for tomorrow?"

"To play with your children, to keep them busy and cheerful so they don't feel lonely."

Marcu's black eyebrows lifted. "Why would they be lonely when they have each other?"

"Because they don't have enough time with you. They'd love to play with you. Cards, chess, checkers, tag."

"I haven't done that in years."

"Exactly my point. Maybe it's time to be a little less distant, and a little more playful.

"Surely, you can remember what it was like to be a boy. You have two little boys who would love it if you'd build a fort with them, or pull out their box of toy soldiers and wage a battle. They'd love to run through the halls and have a sword fight—" She noticed his expression, her lips twisting ruefully. "No, not a real sword fight, but a battle with wooden spoons or broom handles. Better yet, the three of you can make your own swords together. Matteo and Antonio would be over the moon."

"And Rocca, what of her? How shall I entertain her?" he answered mildly.

"A tea party, or a puppet performance—"

"Excuse me?"

"Or a sword fight. Lots of girls like pretending to be sword masters."

"Did you ever once see my sisters run around with swords?"

"That doesn't mean Rocca couldn't." Her eyebrow lifted, matching his expression. "Or do you have fixed ideas about what is proper play for girls and boys?"

"You're trying to be provocative."

"I'm trying to do what you brought me here to do—make sure your children are truly your first priority." She rose and gave him a crooked smile. "Good night, Marcu. I'm glad you're home safe. Sleep well."

She could feel his gaze burning through her back as she headed for the door. He didn't speak until she was reaching for the doorknob.

"I was on my way home to Aosta when I

crashed. I'd already ended things with Vittoria and was coming back here to you—"

"You were not coming back to me," she interrupted firmly, ignoring the quickening of her pulse.

"But I was. I ended things with her because of you."

"No." Monet's heart did another hard double beat. "No, don't say that, because it's not true."

"It absolutely is." He faced her, arms crossed over his broad chest. "I told you I wouldn't touch you again as long as I was in another relationship, and I didn't. But I'm no longer involved with Vittoria—"

"You really hit your head hard today. I think you should lie down."

"You feel the same thing I feel. This attraction isn't one-sided. It killed me keeping my hands off you—"

"I think we should ring for a doctor. You need help."

He rolled his eyes. "Don't be a coward. And don't make me prove my point. There is something between us and I realized a lot of things today. The accident forced me to confront not just my mortality but the future. Why be with someone I don't care about, when I could be with someone like you—"

"No." She flung her hands up, trying to stop him. "We won't ever be together. We don't have a relationship, nor will we ever have one."

He crossed the room, approaching her. "We've had a relationship for years. We've just ignored it. And I'm not going to ignore it anymore."

She edged the other way, moving behind the couch. "What relationship? Marcu, eight years ago I was an eighteen-year-old virgin who idolized you! I had no life experience. I had no sexual experience. Yes, I adored you. I was impossibly infatuated, but that's not the basis for a mature relationship now."

"Why not?"

"One-sided adoration is pathetic."

"I told you, this isn't one-sided. I wouldn't have broken things off with Vittoria if I had no feelings for you—"

"You don't have feelings for me! And you didn't break up with Vittoria for me. I am absolutely inconsequential."

"If that was true, then why did my father fear you so? Why was he afraid of your power over me?"

She leaned on the back of the couch, hands gripping the crushed velvet. "You're not making any sense. You should sit down. You need to rest. I'm worried about you."

"Monet, I have a headache, I haven't lost my mind."

"Then why say your father was afraid of me? How could he be afraid of me? I was almost nineteen when you got married. I had no power."

"My father knew how I felt about you. He knew how upset I was when you left, and that I was conflicted in those months after you'd gone, so conflicted that I booked a flight to go see you in London but I never actually got on the plane, as he kept finding ways to stop me."

"Your father obviously knew best. Galeta was the right one for you."

"I shouldn't have allowed my father to influence my judgment. I've never forgiven myself for that—"

"You say these things as if you're certain I had feelings for you. You say this as if you coming to London would have changed the outcome—"

"Wouldn't it?" he interrupted. "If I had shown

up in London in those first few months, and told you how much I cared about you, you don't think it would have had any impact? You don't think we might have had a real relationship?"

She picked up a cushion from the couch and threw it at him. "*No*. You were never serious about me. You wanted something easy, convenient, and I was there at the palazzo, easy and convenient. But then when I was no longer easy or convenient, I was too much trouble." She grabbed another pillow and threw this one at him, too. He sidestepped the second pillow, just as he had the first.

"I'm not judging you, Marcu, just clarifying facts," she said, wishing there was another pillow to throw. "We were never meant to be. You and I have very different ideas about life, and struggle, and identity. Your whole identity is that of being Matteo Uberto's eldest son. You are the heir. You have royal blood in your DNA—"

"This has nothing to do with us."

"It has everything to do with it. Your ancestry matters to your family, just as your wife's ancestry mattered to your father. I don't come from a family where we brag about our lineage, and I've spent the past eight years trying to carve my identity out, creating one far from my mother's shadow."

"Your mother was a good person, and a beautiful woman."

"And insecure as hell." Monet made a face. "She had a desperate need to be loved—not by me, but by others. She needed your approval more than mine. She needed your brother and sisters' affection more than mine. Why? Because I was hers, and I had to love her. Your family...that was the challenge." She grimaced again. "But why are we talking about the past? It's always about the past. I'm tired of the past. I'm only interested in the present, and the future, which is why I love London. In London everything is new for me. I have interesting work, and a fulfilling life. I never look back, and I never feel like a second-class citizen."

"You've never been a second-class citizen."

She forced a mocking smile to her lips even as she held back the sting of tears. "When it comes to the Ubertos, I've always been a second-class citizen. To quote your father, I'm only 'good enough to bed, but not to wed.' Good night, Marcu."

He followed her out, catching up with her on the stairs. "Monet, wait."

"This isn't a good time for us to talk, Marcu. You've gone through a great deal today. It's been so stressful—"

"I know the kind of day I had today, and it was rough. Twice I thought I make not make it home, but that was also a much-needed wake-up call. Life is short. We're mortal. We don't really have time to waste."

"I'm glad you had an epiphany. But that changes nothing between us."

"I don't want Vittoria. I want you."

"No. *No*." Her laugh was incredulous. "I'm not a replacement for Vittoria. I'm not easy, or convenient. I'm not an option in any way."

"The kiss we shared—"

"Shouldn't have happened."

"But it did, and it made me question everything." He climbed yet another step so that he was just one stair below her now. "I've been determined to go through life without feeling, but that's obviously not working, not for me, or anyone." He took the next stair so that they were side by side. "The children have no idea how much I love them, when everything I do is to ensure their well-being."

He lifted a long tendril of hair from her shoulder, the silky strands sliding through his fingers. "And you—you imagine that you're someone I wanted to use for my pleasure because I had nothing else to do, and no one else to turn to, and that's not true. It's not ever been true."

"Please, Marcu, I'm not a fool. You married Galeta only a few months after I left Palermo. She must have already been on the horizon when you were making love to me in your bedroom."

"We'd dated. We weren't serious."

"Just like you weren't serious with me."

"I never hid anything from you. You knew I was socially active."

She averted her face, features tightening. "This walk down memory lane isn't helping anyone."

"My point is, I've always been honest with you, even when it wasn't easy or comfortable. I am being honest now when I say that kissing you changed something inside of me. It woke something—"

"No."

"But it did, it has." He reached out, tipping her face up, his finger beneath her chin. "I haven't felt anything in years. I've been numb, and then you come back into my life—"

"Because you dragged me back into your life!"

The corner of his mouth lifted. "Okay, that's fair. I did drag you, but I think I finally understand why I had to call in that favor. I needed you."

She drew away from him and climbed a step. "For the children."

"No, not for the children, but for me. I just didn't know it yet."

She climbed another step. "How convenient to realize that after I was here, hostage."

"You're not a hostage. You could go anytime."

Monet turned to face him fully, eyebrows rising, dark wings above brilliant golden-brown eyes. "So if I asked you to let me return home, you'd allow it?"

"Yes."

"If I said I wanted to go tomorrow, you'd be fine with that?"

He felt a pinch in his chest—sharp, hard,

deep. "Yes," he said after a moment, uncertain how they'd come to this place already. He'd fought to come home, fought to return to her, and now she wanted to leave him.

Marcu took a breath, "Yes," he repeated, "but you wouldn't be able to leave tomorrow. You won't be able to go anywhere until the storm passes, and that's another few days."

"Then I want to leave, as soon as I can." Her gaze met his. "Will you agree to that?"

The pinch was even stronger this time, stealing his breath. He didn't want to answer. He had to answer. "Yes."

She seemed to think this over and then she nodded. "Thank you." And then she leaned down and kissed him. "I don't hate you," she whispered against his mouth. "But I can't stay. It's not good for either of us."

And just like that, heat exploded between them, and her light kiss became fire, and the fire was bigger than either of them.

He pulled her to him, holding her firmly while he kissed her deeply, parting her lips with the pressure of his. She made a soft groaning sound, which just whetted his hunger, and his tongue teased the softness of her lower lip before stroking the inside of her mouth. She tasted of almonds and cinnamon and her…how he loved the taste of her. No one had ever felt so right in his arms. No kiss had ever made him feel like this, either.

She reached for him, her arms wrapping around his neck, and the kiss was a mutual give-and-take, the hunger binding them together. Her fingers threaded in his hair, and he shuddered with pleasure at the feel of her fingertips across his nape.

"Take me to your room," she breathed. "Let's not do this where everyone can see."

He swung her into his arms and carried her up the remaining flight of stairs to his suite. She was light in his arms, her body soft and warm, and he tried not to get ahead of himself. She hadn't offered herself up. She hadn't promised anything. This was just a kiss, and he could be satisfied with that because he wanted her to be happy. It was time he made her happy.

She felt like she'd waited for this moment—and him—for her whole life, and she had no fear as he undressed her.

He was the one for her, and the one she wanted

to be with now. She wasn't going to think about the future, or the past, she was simply going to give herself over to the pleasure of being with Marcu, the man she adored. Life was complicated and hard and she should be able to have this moment for her, to remember forever.

Stripped bare, he studied her a long moment and then kissed her mouth, and the side of her neck, and beneath her ear in that delicate hollow where every nerve ending seemed to be.

His mouth traveled down the length of her neck, his tongue flicking her collarbone—more nerves, more tingling sensations that made her tremble and ache.

He took his time exploring her curves and shape, lips and tongue and teeth on her nipples, then strokes of his tongue to soothe the light bites. Her breasts felt full and ripe, her nipples strained. She struggled to catch her breath, dazed by the sharp hot sensations filling her veins, coiling in her belly.

He continued his exploration, moving lower, dropping kisses to her belly button and on each hip bone, fingers light across her pelvis, grazing her inner thighs.

She closed her eyes, panting as he parted her

thighs, pressing her knees down, open, revealing her most private place. It was terrifying and exhilarating all at the same time because this was so new and yet it felt so good, and it was him, Marcu, who was making her feel this way. Hot, alive, glorious.

His hands parted her thighs wider and then his mouth was there, and his tongue traced the delicate folds. She shuddered at every light lick, unbearably sensitive, her insides feeling like hot thick honey. She was wet and growing wetter, and his fingers slid into her even as he teased her clit, his breath warm, his tongue cool. He lifted his head to watch her as he stroked her with his fingers, burying himself in her tight heat, and it was strange, but wonderful. She bucked as he dropped his head to kiss her nub as he continued stroking her, the incredible sensations flooding her, building, rising higher and higher until she went over an edge, and shattered into a thousand bright pieces.

She lay boneless, heart still pounding, body still tingling, her skin still exquisitely sensitive. It took her a moment to collect herself. "That was nice," she said huskily, "but I want you."

"We don't need—"

"No, we don't need to do anything, but I want everything. I want you. I've wanted this since I was eighteen."

"You're sure?"

"Absolutely," she answered, reaching out to clasp his thick erection, savoring the feel of his hard silken shaft in her hand.

He reached for protection and rolled the condom down before moving over her, his knees holding her thighs open. He lowered himself on his elbows, and kissed her even as the head of his shaft pressed against her slick entrance.

She nearly told him to take it slow, and then she held the words back, because she didn't want to make this about her virginity, but about him, *them*.

He was sliding into her, and the fullness was overwhelming. She had to force herself to breathe and relax, as his body pressed deeper into hers. She wasn't sure she liked it, he felt too big, and too uncomfortable, and just when she didn't think she could do this anymore, the pain eased, and the fullness was less overwhelming and as he moved, she felt a fluttering sensation, a lovely fluttering sensation that made her want to feel it again. She arched her hips against his and he withdrew slightly, stroking back in. The lovely fluttery sensation was amazing and she urged him on, loving the heat of his body, the feel of his warmth within her, surrounding her, making her safe…making her his.

He kissed her the way his body loved hers—deep, hungry, commanding—and she loved it all.

And when she climaxed again, he was there with her, too, and it was bliss. No matter what happened next, no matter what happened in the future, she was grateful to have had this time in Marcu's arms, in his bed, in his life.

Monet woke slowly, trying to get her bearings. It was extremely early in the morning and the sky was still dark outside. And then she shifted and bumped into Marcu's shoulder and it all came back to her.

She was in Marcu's room. They'd made love last night. He'd given her two orgasms and she was most definitely no longer without experience.

She also needed to use his bathroom, desperately. Monet slid from the bed and went to his en-suite bathroom, returning quietly, hoping that Marcu was still asleep. Instead he was frowning at the bottom sheet on her side of the bed.

"Did I hurt you?" he asked gruffly, exposing the red stain.

"No," she answered, mortified.

"But I made you bleed."

"I'll get a washcloth and some soap—"

"I'm not worried about the stain. I'm worried about you. I didn't realize I was so rough with you."

She didn't know how to tell him, so she just blurted the words. "You weren't rough. I was a virgin."

"What?"

She ignored his growl of shock. "Everyone has to have a first time. It's not a biggie."

"You should have told me!"

"Why? How did it matter?"

"I would have been far more careful."

"You were wonderful. I have no complaints." Her lips curved. "Honest."

He left the bed naked, and stared at her, expression incredulous. "I had no idea."

"That I was a virgin? Why does it matter?"

"It doesn't. But I just assumed—" He broke off, scowling. "I would have thought by now you'd have more…experience."

"No. I don't date very much, haven't been interested. But I have no regrets, giving up my virginity to you. It only seems fitting that my first time be with you."

He covered his face with his hand. *"Mio Dio."*

"Stop with the dramatic curses. Why does it matter that I was a virgin? I wanted to sleep with you, and I'm glad I did. It was amazing for a first time. You've set the bar very high."

His hand fell from his face and he glared at her from across the width of the bed. "What does that mean?"

"I've lacked confidence since I am—was—inexperienced, but maybe now I'll be more confident, and comfortable. Maybe dating won't be such a big deal. Hopefully I'll be more open to meeting new men."

"That doesn't make any sense," he snapped, heading to the bathroom, and returning in a black thick robe. He was knotting the sash as he emerged.

"Maybe not to you, but it does to me. It's time

I let go of the past and move forward. It's time I gave others a chance—"

"No."

She arched a brow as she sat back down in bed and pulled the covers up to her chest. "You can't tell me no."

"I don't want you to give others a chance. I want you. I want you to stay with us."

She watched him give his sash a second angry knot. "It doesn't work that way."

"Why not?"

"You're being ridiculous now. Don't ask questions like that. Because I don't belong here. This isn't my home. You're not my family. And I have no desire to be your glorified child care for the rest of my life!"

"I still have Miss Sheldon as a nanny. You aren't meant to be child care."

"You wanted a wife to handle your children so you could focus on work. I've no intention of touching any of that. Find another woman who wants that responsibility because it's not going to be me."

"You're not even giving me a chance!"

"Marcu, I just spent the night with you. I gave

you my body. I gave you my virginity. How have I not given you a chance?"

"Marry me."

Now he was just being cruel. Or was this his idea of being funny? Sighing, she tossed back the covers and began to gather her clothes. "Never mind. I can't listen to this. I need to go."

He blocked her, catching her hands in his. "I'm serious. Marry me. Stay with us. We need you."

His words did weird things to her insides—both good and bad. "Marry me, stay with us" made her heart jump, but "we need you" filled her with mistrust. She struggled to shake him off, desperately wanting to be dressed and in her own room. "That is the worst proposal I've ever heard and I'm going to pretend you didn't say any of it. Now give me space, so I can dress and get out of here."

Instead he pulled her into his arms, and kissed her, a hot, hard punishing kiss that sent a molten wave of longing through her. His hand was low on her bare back, making her body tingle, and as he swept his palm up over her spine, she shuddered with pleasure. He made her feel so sensitive and alive, and when he cupped the back of her head, holding her still so that he could deepen the kiss, all she could think about was him, and having him inside her again, filling her, making them one. When he was with her, making love to her, she'd never felt more connected, or more loved—

And suddenly she flashed back in time, to when she was just a little girl and she'd accidentally walked in on her mother in bed with a stout older man.

She'd been shocked and confused.

She didn't understand who the man was, and why he was in her mother's bed. She didn't understand why her mother spent more time with strange men than with her.

Desire squashed, Monet pulled back, and Marcu released her, letting her take one step back and then another until there was ample distance between them.

She struggled to regain control, struggled to calm her breathing. Marcu's eyes were narrowed, his expression inscrutable. Monet felt stupid tears burn the back of her eyes. "I hate your proposal. I hate how it demeans me," she choked.

"Because I don't have a ring? I didn't get

down on one knee? I wasn't going to get down on one knee with Vittoria—"

"I don't care about Vittoria. Or about Galeta. I don't care about any of your women. I care about me, and what you're offering me and it's nothing—"

"How can you say that? I would take care of you, and provide for you, and you'd never want for anything."

"But love." She blinked hard, fighting the scalding tears. "Because where is the love? There is no love in any of this. There is desire and want and the physical attraction between us is incredible. The sex was unbelievable. I will never regret that you were my first lover. It was right." She reached up to swipe away one tear, and then another. "It's what probably should have happened eight years ago so I could have gotten you out of my system. But now we have been together and we've come full circle. I can move on. We are good."

"We are not good," he snapped. "We are most certainly not good. I did not take your virginity only for you to walk away—"

She laughed and kept laughing, and it was making him mad but she couldn't help it, and she couldn't stop. Her laughter turned into help-less giggles. "Oh, Marcu, what did you think would happen? That sex with you would make me give up my whole life? My dreams—"

"Of working in a department store?"

"It's actually something I enjoy so don't you dare mock me!"

He rubbed his hands over his face and growled with frustration. "I'm not mocking you, I'm trying to understand how you could choose that life over one with me and the children?"

"I realize marriage for you is a business deal, but it's not my idea of marriage, and I don't need a man. I need independence. I need self-respect. I need my own path."

"So what was this? What happened here?"

"I wanted you. I have wanted to be with you since I was eighteen. And so I slept with you, and I did it mostly for closure. I slept with you so that—" She broke off abruptly, unwilling to say what was burning in her heart.

So that I would always have this moment with you. So that I would always have this memory.

This was her secret, not his. Her memory for her to cherish, and she would cherish it, but he didn't need to know that making love with him was bittersweet. He didn't need to know that being so close to him had been heaven, and it would hurt like hell to walk away, but far better to leave and hurt and heal, then stay and be overlooked day in and day out.

"Finish your sentence," he said curtly. "I'm hanging on your every word. I'm trying to understand."

"There is nothing to understand. I wanted to be in your bed. I wanted to make love to you. I did. We did. And now I'm ready to go as soon as the storm lets up."

He crossed his arms, and his jaw jutted. "I don't like any of this."

"I know you don't, but you'll be fine the moment I'm gone and you reach back out to Vittoria, or you set your sights on the next appropriate woman. I'm just convenient, Marcu. Don't forget that."

"That's a terrible thing to say."

"But true," she said, tugging her sweater over her head, and crumpling the rest of her clothes into a ball. "This isn't complicated between us. We both had an itch to scratch, and we scratched it, freeing you to find the next aristocratic young woman with the bloodline you desire." And then she tried to put on her knit slacks but Marcu scooped her into his arms and carried her back to the bed.

"Then why isn't my itch scratched?" he asked, pinning her to the bed. "Why do I just want even more of you?"

"Because you like what you can't have."

"But I can have you. I know if I told you how much I wanted you right now, and how much I ache to be inside of you, and how much I want to taste you, you'd welcome all of it." He pressed her hands open, and placed his palm flat against hers in a slow caress. "And if I'm wrong, tell me right now, and I'll let you go and we will be done with the itch and the scratch and all of it, because I do want you, but I want you to want me, too."

There was so much heat and energy zinging between them. Just the press of his palm to hers made her want to arch up against him.

Was it bad that she loved being pinned to the bed like this? Was it bad that the sheer strength of him made her shivery and excited?

"I do want you," she answered, throwing her head back, which resulted in him dropping his head, and kissing the side of her neck, his lips setting her on fire.

"Then stay," he said huskily. "Because I want you here, *la mia bella ragazza.*"

His beautiful girl.

She closed her eyes as he kissed her, and gave him the rest of her heart because there was no one else she'd rather give it to. There was no one she'd rather be with. She'd never wanted anyone but him. But she just couldn't let him know she loved him.

She couldn't ever give him that power over her.

CHAPTER NINE

A FEW HOURS later Monet was woken by the most lovely sensation of his hand stroking her side, and then up her rib cage to cup her breast. Of course her nipple pebbled and he stroked that, too, all while she pretended to still be sleeping, wanting to just focus on how he made her body feel.

He made her body feel amazing.

But it was harder to feign sleep when he tugged on her nipple and flooded her with warmth, making her ache between her thighs, making her want him deep inside of her again.

And still, she kept her eyes closed, focusing on his warm palm against her breast, and the thick length of his erection against her backside.

Her body was waking everywhere and it was almost painful not responding. She wanted to turn over and give him all of her...well, all but her heart, because she didn't trust him with that.

"I know you're awake," he murmured, his breath warm against her neck.

She smiled into her pillow. "Mmm...?"

"You're a faker," he answered, sliding his hand lower, down over her hip, the curve of her butt, before slipping between her thighs. "So wet," he said, stroking her.

She gasped as he touched her; she was wet, and ready for him. She rolled onto her back and reached for him. He kissed her, and moved between her thighs but didn't enter her. Instead he leaned back and reached for a condom and sheathed himself before burying himself inside of her.

Monet sighed with pleasure as he filled her. He was big and the fullness was somewhat overwhelming and then it was perfect.

She linked her hands behind his neck and pulled him down to her, so she could kiss him as he thrust into her. This was exactly what she needed—him, all of him. It wasn't just sex, but joy at the deepest level. To finally know him, to finally be able to express her love for him... if not in words, then in actions. The climax was shattering, and even more bruising for her heart because the more she cared, the more the pleasure hurt.

Afterward she lay across his chest, in the hazy afterglow, thoughts drifting, emotions still not quite in control.

Leaving him would be so brutal.

Forgetting him would be impossible.

"This is why I came back," he said quietly, playing with her hair, the long strands slipping through his fingers. "I came back for you."

"Marcu," she protested huskily, a lump forming in her throat. "Let's not talk about that again."

"Why not? It's true. You're here because I needed you, and not for the children, but for me. I didn't see it before, but it hit me as I was leaving the *castello* yesterday. I didn't even want to get in the car, and once I was driving away, I felt almost sick. I didn't want to leave you, nor did I want to spend Christmas away from all of you. This was where I wanted to be—with you, and my children."

She sat up to see his face. "Don't mistake desire for love, or affection. It's not the basis for commitment, nor will it provide stability for a family of young children."

He said nothing for a moment. "Are you afraid of commitment?"

Her cheeks flamed with heat and her pulse thudded hard. Her body still felt treacherously warm, and aware. *"No!"*

"Then why can't we discuss us?"

"Because that's not why I slept with you!" She left the bed and reached for the soft cashmere throw on a chair near his hearth, and wrapped it around her. "I slept with you because I found you appealing, and yes, I was curious as to what making love with you would be like, and it was wonderful. But at the same time, I have no interest in pursuing this further. What we did together was lovely, and I have no regrets about losing my virginity to you, but once I leave, it's over."

"Why?"

"Why wouldn't it be? I came to Aosta to take care of your children, not play the part of your mistress. I might be my mother's daughter, but I have too much self-respect to go down that path."

"Our parents loved each other."

She let out a strangled laugh and pulled the fuzzy blanket closer to her bare shoulders. "I wouldn't ever call it that," she said hoarsely, remembering the inequality in their relationship. Matteo Uberto had all the power. Her mother had none.

"My father proposed to her twice. She turned him down both times."

She'd heard this before, from her mother, but she hadn't believed her. Monet had thought her mother was telling her what she thought Monet wanted to hear. "And yet he replaced her with a younger model when she turned forty."

Marcu sat up, the covers falling low to his hips, revealing his lean, muscular torso. "Because your mother was ill and she kept the news from my father, not wanting him to see her sick. She left him, not the other way around."

"That's not true!"

"But it is. My father loved your mother. And he didn't replace her with a younger model. There was never anyone else for him, not after she died."

His words caught her off guard and Monet stiffened, before turning away. Was that true? Or was Marcu twisting the past, changing facts into something less unsavory? She gave her head a shake, unsettled.

"It doesn't matter," she said after a moment, crossing the room to stand at Marcu's bedroom window. He hadn't closed the shutters last night and in the early morning light one could see the snow still falling, piling high on the stone ledge and coating the thick glass. "You brought me to Aosta so you could spend time alone with Vittoria before you proposed to her. That was our understanding. It's why I dropped everything to come to Italy. I'm here expressly to manage the children, and that agreement has not changed." She paused, and turned to look at Marcu, her gaze meeting his. "Nor do I want it to change. Despite the incredible lovemaking."

"So what happens now?" he asked grimly.

"I shower and dress and prepare for a day with the children, and you do what you would ordinarily do."

"I'd like to spend it with the children."

Again, he'd caught her off guard. She nodded approvingly, even if she felt somewhat off balance. "Good. They'd love that."

"And I'd like to spend the day with you, too… all of us together."

"They need time with you, without me there."

His mouth opened, then closed. He nodded. "You're right. Take the day off."

"You mean the morning, or the afternoon?"

"No, I mean the whole day." He paused. "You do get days off at Bernard's, don't you?"

"Of course I do."

"Then enjoy having some time to yourself."

She did enjoy having the morning to herself, but by early afternoon Monet was bored and restless. She couldn't stop thinking about last night, and how she'd spent it in Marcu's bed.

She might be conflicted about some things, but she had no confusion about how he made her feel, especially when she was in his arms, her body pressed to his. There was something magical about his skin against her skin and his mouth on hers. She loved his warmth and his strength, she loved the way he smelled and how incredible his touch made her feel. She came alive in his arms—everything within her screamed to life at the brush of his lips. There were moments when she thought she would give up everything for more of this, and more time with Marcu. She'd sacrifice future security for more happiness right now, but inevitably reason would intrude, and reality would return and she'd scold herself for being foolish. She couldn't afford to be a romantic. Couldn't afford to be stupid. She might want Marcu more than she'd ever wanted anyone, but he didn't love her. He only wanted her, and when the physical desire eventually faded—and it always did, just look at her mother—what would she be left with? Nothing.

Marcu took the children outside after breakfast to build snowmen, and then they had a snowball fight, with Matteo and Antonio battling Marcu and Rocca. The snow had stopped falling for the present, but the storm wasn't over and clouds hung low in the sky.

After the snowball fight they all took warm baths and changed into dry clothes before having lunch, and then relaxed in the music room, where the kids took turns playing the piano. Only Matteo had had lessons but the younger ones wanted to try to play, and Marcu sat down with Antonio and listened to him pound on the keys for a bit until Marcu said he wanted to play something. The children looked so shocked that it jolted Marcu's complacency and it crossed his mind that Monet was right. His children didn't really know him, not anymore.

"You know I play piano," he said, playing a simple melody with his right hand.

The children all shook their heads.

"I used to play a lot," he added. "I loved music. I wanted to study music but your grand-father said it wouldn't pay the bills. So I gave up my music studies when I went to university."

"Play us something then, Papà," Antonio said, still perched on the piano bench next to him.

Marcu thought a moment and then began to play something he'd learned years ago, and even though he hadn't touched the piano since before Galeta died, his fingers remembered the notes, and he just let himself play, lost in the song and the moment, because it was a special moment, having his three children with him, all riveted to the medieval Italian Christmas carol.

Marcu smiled at his children when he finished. "What did you think?"

"Beautiful," said Rocca.

"I didn't know you knew Christmas songs," Matteo said.

"I'd forgotten that one," Marcu answered truthfully, aware that once again Monet had been right. She was opening his eyes and he didn't like what he was seeing. Despite his best intentions, he had failed his children.

"Can you play us something else?" Rocca asked.

He thought for a moment and then began to play an aria from Puccini. Monet had loved Puccini. She'd discovered a passion for opera when she'd lived at the palazzo, and Marcu had gone out and bought DVDs for her of all the great operas, but Puccini remained her favorite composer.

When he finished, the children begged for another song but he shook his head and stood up. "Maybe later. Now I think we go up to the nursery and let you have a short rest before dinner."

"Will you read to us while we rest?" Rocca caught his hand and held it while they left the room. "Signorina Wilde always reads to us."

"She's been reading us *The Nutcracker*," Antonio added. "I like the Mouse King."

"And I like Clara. She's lovely." Rocca skipped next to him as they started up the stairs. "And she gets to have a Christmas ball. I wish we could have one."

"A Christmas ball?" Marcu's brow creased as he glanced down at his daughter. "You don't even know what a ball is, do you?"

"It's where everyone dresses up and they dance and have a huge party, and we have a ballroom here, so we could have one."

"We do have a ballroom," he agreed. "But who would we invite? We know no one here. Everyone in our family is in Palermo."

"But there are lots of people in the village, and we have everyone who works here, and their families. Why don't we invite them to come to our party?"

"It sounds like a lot of effort, and a lot of money," Marcu answered, more to himself than her.

"But it would be fun, and you have a lot of money," she retorted, giving his hand a squeeze. "And it would make everyone happy. Don't you think it would make them happy to come here for a big party?"

He smoothed the tip of her ponytail. "I don't know. That's a good question."

"Well, I think they'd be happy. Especially if we had a big tree like Clara had, and toys and lots of cookies and music." She hesitated, then added in a rush, "And Signorina would like it, too. She said she loves Christmas and in London everything has lights and pretty decorations. Wouldn't it be fun to surprise her and make it look like London here?"

Marcu choked back a laugh. "Well, we couldn't make it look like London, but we could probably organize something in the ballroom and celebrate the holidays with our staff."

"And everyone in the village."

"A few people from the village."

"And the farmer who brought you home."

"*Va bene*, and the farmer who brought me home."

Rocca smiled delightedly. "I can't wait to tell Signorina!"

"What if we don't tell her? What if we make it a surprise?"

Rocca frowned and looked at her brothers and then back at her father, a deep crease between her brows. "That's a terrible idea, Papà. She has to be dressed up, too. How can she come to a ball without a special dress?"

He couldn't stifle the laugh this time. "You make an excellent point, but let's not say anything to her yet because I'm not sure if we can make this happen."

"Why not?"

"We'd need the staff's help and I'm sure they're busy getting ready for their Christmas, too."

"So let's do it before Christmas Eve."

"That's only days from now."

Rocca was not easily discouraged. "Or Christmas day?"

Marcu checked his smile. "Let me ask the staff. If they are to be our guests, shouldn't we find out what day they'd like to come to a party?"

That evening Monet wasn't able to hear what Marcu and the children were talking about in the nursery, but she knew he'd gone up with them to put them to bed and he'd stayed in the nursery for forty-five minutes. She wondered if the children said prayers, or if he'd told them a story. She was glad he was with them, though, and glad she'd decided to accept their invitation and join them for dinner as everyone had looked happy and relaxed, and the children had teased Marcu and he'd teased them right back.

She hadn't stayed for dessert but went up to her room to take a bath and get ready for bed. She tried to read but couldn't focus on the words, and then she took out a bottle of nail polish and touched up her toenails. Monet glanced at the clock on the wall every now and then, noting that a half hour had passed, and then an hour, since Marcu had left the nursery and gone down the stairs.

She waited until another half hour passed before leaving her room to go downstairs to his bedroom. She wasn't sure what he'd say when he opened his door. Fortunately, he didn't keep her waiting. He simply opened his door wide and stepped back. That was all the invitation she needed.

After closing the door behind her, he swept her into his arms and carried her to the bed, where he slowly undressed her, taking time to kiss each inch of skin he bared.

She sighed and shivered as he kissed his way from her throat, to her collarbone, to her breasts, and tummy, and then finally between her legs. He settled there, too, and kissed and sucked and licked for an impossibly long time, making her arch and cry his name until he finally gave her the release she craved.

They made love twice, and she fell asleep curled against him, but now it was almost morning and she was wide-awake and still lying in his arms, but she felt restless and anxious and as she struggled to not think, or feel too much, tears started to her eyes.

This was madness coming to his room. She shouldn't have done it, but she couldn't stay away. She'd wanted him, and this, and he'd more than satisfied her last night, but now she felt sad, as well as strangely empty.

Monet pressed her cheek to his warm chest and blinked back tears. If only she didn't care for him. If only her feelings for him had been purely physical and making love with him could have satisfied her. Instead it had teased her heart, opening her to emotions she wasn't prepared to face.

She'd loved him since she was just a girl. She couldn't imagine ever loving anyone but him. But Marcu didn't love her back. Marcu would be able to take care of her, and give her enormous pleasure, but he'd never give her what she needed most—love. Endless, boundless love.

"What are you thinking about?" Marcu's deep voice broke the silence.

She wiggled closer to him. "Nothing."

"I can feel the weight of your thoughts. You can talk to me. Tell me what is worrying you."

But she couldn't talk to him. She didn't want to change what was between them—the intimacy was lovely, and special, as well as fleeting. It wouldn't last. Which is why she wanted to treasure it as long as she could. "I think I'm just tired. We don't sleep much when we're together."

He laughed softly, and stroked her hair, and then her back, his caress a comfort and a pleasure. "Then sleep."

It had taken her a while, but Monet was sleeping now, curled close to his side. Marcu was glad she slept, but he couldn't. He was lying on his back, an arm behind his head, staring at the ceiling, chest tight with bottled air.

It hurt to breathe. His head ached. He couldn't ease the pressure in his chest, while the difficult conversations with Monet played endlessly in his head.

She said he'd never mentioned love to her,

and it was true. Love. Such a difficult concept for him.

He'd spent the past few days trying to figure out what love would look like, feel like. He loved his children, but even that was restrained and controlled. For him, love was duty and responsibility, love was loyalty. Had he ever truly been in love?

He'd married Galeta because it was a smart decision, a good decision, and so it had proved to be in that they suited each other and had a strong marriage. He had been prepared to marry Vittoria because he'd considered that she would make a good wife and mother. He'd never felt any desire for Vittoria. She was a beautiful woman but he felt nothing resembling need, hunger, passion. The only person he had ever truly wanted like that had been Monet. But had that desire, that craving, been love? Or was it, as Monet said, just lust?

He tried to think back, tried to remember who he'd been eight years ago. He'd changed so much it was hard to think back without some scorn because he'd been so much softer then, so unrealistic. He'd wanted Monet badly. He wanted her not just in a sexual sense but in a keep-her-close, and keep-her-safe way.

She'd felt like his. His family, his home, his heart. No one knew him better. No one had talked to him more, or listened more. No one had smiled the way she'd smiled when he entered a room. Her face would light up, her eyes would grow bright. She'd radiated warmth and sweetness, energy and light. She'd made him think of orange blossoms and honey and sunshine.

Had that been love?

Had what he felt then been love, but he hadn't known it? And yet how could he not know?

How could he go through a life without love?

How could he not know how to express love?

Did his children not feel loved by him?

What was his problem with love? Was it the word, or the action?

Or both?

Marcu eased away from Monet, put his robe on and went upstairs to the nursery to check on the children. They were all sound asleep, each in a different position. Rocca slept sideways, Matteo was straight as an arrow, and Antonio was a little ball.

He went from bed to bed, straightening covers, pressing a quick hand to a small warm head, and each time he felt a twinge in his chest, adding to the ache already there.

What had happened to him since Galeta died?

But also, what had happened to him before he married Galeta to make a practical marriage so appealing to him? Surely it wasn't just his father's influence? His father had only had so much influence over him.

Then what?

Marcu knew he was more reserved than his younger brother and sisters. He was old enough to remember the day his mother left, and yet young enough to miss her profoundly. But he'd always been more reserved, hadn't he?

Or had losing her at twelve changed him? Hardened him? Numbed him? Made it more difficult for him to feel—and give—love?

He wished he knew, and tonight as he went back around the nursery once more, to kiss each child on the forehead, he felt as if his chest was full of hot sharp shards of glass.

He did love his children, very much. He simply struggled to show the depth of his feelings.

Worse, he struggled just feeling feelings.

But that didn't mean he couldn't try to express them. And he would. He had a plan—it'd take some work…but he could do it.

He would do it.

Monet woke up to blinding sunshine. Warm golden light flooded the room, illuminating the floor and warming the bed. For a moment she couldn't get her bearings and then she realized she was in Marcu's room, and from the light pouring through the window, it was late.

She sat up, and glanced around, discovering Marcu in sweatpants and a knit shirt, reading in a chair by the fire. "What time is it?" she asked, running a hand through her long hair, trying to smooth the tangles.

"Almost nine."

"Nine? The children!"

"Elise is with them. We're sleeping in and in moments we'll be having a lovely breakfast here together."

"In your room?"

"In my bed."

She blushed. "It's daylight. I can't be here. If I'm caught having breakfast here, then the staff knows we've been together."

"And you don't think they've known you slept in here the last two nights?"

"No," she said, thinking they'd been quite clever and stealthy.

"There are cameras in the corridors," he said, "for security."

"Oh."

"And then there were the sheets."

Monet closed her eyes, mortified. It was embarrassing to realize that everyone knew what she and Marcu had been doing. "I can't imagine what they're thinking."

"I don't really care."

"But I do," she said, throwing back the covers, to get her robe and gown, because the vexing thing was, she really did care. Having grown up listening to people whisper about her mother, Monet didn't like being the subject of anyone's conversation. She'd spent her whole life trying to avoid gossip and speculation.

He rose from his chair and peeled his sweater off and carried it to her. "Put this on instead, it's warm and will cover you as breakfast will be arriving soon."

She frowned at him but did it, and crawled back into bed. "Is this your normal routine?"

"No."

"Have you had many women stay over here?"

"None."

That gave her pause. "What about in Palermo?"

"No one has ever stayed over at any of my family homes. I conduct my private life elsewhere."

"You mean in hotels?"

He sighed. "Monet, you're not like other women. And you are not convenient. You are actually most inconvenient as you demand things of me that no one else demands. You want things I have stopped believing in. You force me to rethink everything I have viewed as truth."

For a moment she couldn't reply, was too busy processing his words and wondering what they truly meant. Was he trying to placate her? If only she didn't doubt him.

They were interrupted by a knock on the door, and Marcu pulled on a shirt and went to open the door. One of the kitchen staff carried in a huge tray and placed it on a side table before leaving. Breakfast was cappuccinos and a basket of warm rolls and fluffy scrambled eggs. Monet didn't think she was hungry and yet she ate everything on her plate, and then had an additional roll with butter and jam.

"This was most indulgent," she said with a sigh, stretching. "Thank you."

He took her hand and carried it to his mouth, kissing her knuckles, and then turned her hand over, his lips brushing the inside of her tender wrist. "If you were my wife, we could do this every weekend."

"Marcu, don't start on that again."

"Why not? I think we should discuss it, seriously—"

"No. It's not right, and it's not real, and to be perfectly honest, this isn't even about me. You don't really want me—"

"But I do. I want you. I don't even know what that means other than I want you in my life, I want you in my home, I want you to be part of my future."

"And your children? How do they play into this?"

"You like my children."

She drew her hand away, and pressed it to her chest, trying to slow the wild beating of her heart. "I *adore* your children, Marcu, but the last thing they need is confusion. And our relationship would confuse them, just as you confuse me." She drew another short painful breath. "You told me in London you didn't even want a wife. You told me you were marrying Vittoria just because you needed someone for the kids—"

"And you said that was the wrong reason to marry. You said, hire better child care," he said.

"Yes."

"And you're right. I don't need you for my children. I need you for me. I need you, Monet. I can imagine a future without you, but I don't like it. I don't want that future. I want a future with you."

She climbed off the bed and shook her head, feeling trapped and cornered and overwhelmed. "I have to go," she said under her breath. "It's time to go."

"The roads aren't clear yet."

"They will be, soon."

"It'll take a day, maybe two."

"What about your helicopter?"

"They have to plow the roads to get to the helipad. That's still a fifteen-to-twenty-minute drive from here."

She closed her eyes, hands in tight fists. "As soon as the weather permits, I would like to leave."

"Understood."

"I also ask that you say nothing to the children. They do not need to be part of this."

"Agreed."

"And when I do go, you must reassure them that I loved spending time with them, and that I am only going so that their Miss Sheldon can return."

"If that is the script...?"

She hated his mocking tone. It only flamed her temper. "You dragged me into this."

"Yes, I did, and I'd keep you here, kicking and screaming, if it was the Middle Ages, but it's not, so I will return you to London as soon as I can."

"Good." She found her nightgown and robe and picked them up. "And we won't do this again...we can't. The children won't understand, and it would only confuse them if they discovered me here with you."

"Whatever you think best," he said, watching her from his side of the bed.

"I don't appreciate your sarcasm."

"I'm sure you don't. Monet Wilde is clever and independent. She needs no man, and she's certainly no pushover."

She stiffened in outrage. "I don't need a man, no. And I don't need a minder, or a keeper, or someone to think for me. I'm not my mother—"

"Mio Dio," he snapped, flinging back the covers and leaving bed. "Not this again."

"You seem to think—"

"No! You seem to think, or fear, that you are like her. You are not like her. You have never been like her, and that's neither criticism or praise. It's just a statement of fact. You are you, and Candie was Candie and I would never ever confuse you for her, not for a second."

Monet bit into her lower lip to keep it from quivering. "I think the less I have to do with you until I leave, the better."

"Fine."

"I'll go see to the children now."

"I wish you would."

CHAPTER TEN

MONET SAW NEXT to nothing of Marcu for the rest of the day, as well as much of the following day, which was Christmas Eve and yet one wouldn't know it from the lack of festivities.

Monet had done her best to keep the children entertained and happy. Yesterday they'd built snow people—because Rocca didn't believe they should be called snowmen when she only made snow girls—and this morning they'd gone sledding. After lunch they'd bundled up again and returned outside to go ice skating on the frozen pond behind the *castello*.

They'd just laced up their skates when Marcu suddenly appeared at the pond, with his own skates. He looked dashing in his black parka.

Monet's heart jumped at the sight of him, and her hands shook as she finished tightening Antonio's skates.

"I've got that," Marcu said, lifting Antonio's skate to adjust the knot.

Monet silently moved away, leaving him to tie the other skate.

Rocca clapped her hands with pleasure, thrilled to have her father with them. The children swarmed Marcu as he got on the ice with them and Monet kept her distance, letting Marcu and the children play.

Everyone skated for an hour before Marcu said it was time to go back to the *castello* and warm up. As they entered the *castello* they discovered that the staff had prepared a treat— hot chocolate and cookies awaited them—and again Monet hung back, feeling strange. She'd told him yesterday that she didn't want to have anything to do with him, and yet she'd thought of him endlessly and missed his company. It was even worse when he was near and they weren't speaking, or looking at each other.

"Time for you to bathe and change," Marcu said to the children. "It's Christmas Eve and we'll have our traditional dinner in two hours in the dining room."

The children smiled hopefully at each other as Monet steered them from the room. "You're welcome to join us," Marcu said casually. "But if our traditions make you uncomfortable, I understand."

Monet turned in the doorway. "I spent six years with your family in Sicily. Six Christmases and never once was I uncomfortable."

"*Bene*. I'll see you with the children in two hours."

The Christmas Eve dinner was exactly as she remembered from Palermo—the same dishes, the same aromas, the same flavors—stirring past memories, and making her think of Sicily, and the lovely times she'd had there, as well as memories of her mother. She'd loved her mother, but it had been such a complicated relationship. Maybe that was okay. Maybe love was complicated and that was okay, too.

She sipped her wine and listened to Marcu and the children talk, and then after the dessert—again, an Uberto favorite from Palermo—they went to the music room and Marcu shocked her by sitting at the piano and playing songs for the children, and not just any songs, but Christmas carols.

The children didn't seem surprised to see him at the piano. They gathered around him and Antonio leaned against his father as Marcu's fingers moved deftly over the keys. And then he began to sing, and she blinked hard, fighting a wave of emotion, thinking she hadn't heard this song in years and years. It was an old carol, a haunting Italian carol, and it filled her with tenderness.

Marcu and the children would be fine. Marcu loved his children. She didn't have to worry about any of them.

And then it was time for bed, and Marcu said he'd walk his children up to the nursery and tell them a story and listen to their prayers.

Monet nodded, and smiled, happy for them. "Good night," she murmured. *"Buon Natale,"* she said as they parted at the nursery door.

"Buon Natale," the children chorused.

Marcu gave her a peculiar look but said nothing and she went to her room, and prepared for bed, and then fought tears for the next hour before she finally fell asleep.

Monet's breakfast arrived on a tray the next morning, carried to her room by Marcu. She hastily dragged a hand through her messy hair, smoothing it. "Good morning," she said huskily.

"Buon Natale," he said, placing the tray on

the table in front of her couch. "I see you have the lights on your little Christmas tree plugged in."

"I've enjoyed my tree very much."

"I'm glad." He hesitated. "We're having a party here, later this afternoon," he added carelessly, as if it was nothing out of the ordinary. "The guests will be arriving at four. The children have party clothes in the nursery if you don't mind helping them dress before."

"Of course I don't," she answered, astonished. "And when did you decide to have this party?"

"Over the weekend."

"You never mentioned it before."

"I wasn't sure if the weather would hold, and I didn't want them disappointed."

He gave her a pointed look. "This was Rocca's idea. Apparently you've been reading *The Nutcracker* to my children, and Rocca very much wants to be Clara."

Monet's lips curved in reluctant amusement. "I do sometimes read the story two or three times a day."

"And she's learned it by heart. Trying to create a Russian fantasy in this *castello* in the midst of the worst winter storm in years hasn't been easy."

Monet couldn't believe what she was hearing. "And yet you're doing it."

"Trying. I don't know if anyone from the village will come, but they have all been invited, and my staff have been invited, along with their families, and I think it should be fun."

Fun. He'd just used the word *fun*. Last night he'd played the piano and sung carols. Today he was throwing a party and talking about fun. "The children know, though," she said slowly.

"The children know I've invited people, and they know the staff have been cleaning and cooking, but they haven't seen the ballroom yet. We've tried to spruce it up a bit, and add a little festive color."

Monet's chest grew warm and she felt a pinch of sharp emotion. "The fact that you tried to do something for them is wonderful. You will have made your children happy, your Rocca most of all."

He fell silent for a moment. "She adores you, you know."

"I adore her, too."

He gave her another long look then walked

from the room. Monet exhaled slowly, painfully, as she heard the door close behind him.

The day passed slowly for everyone, but finally it was midafternoon. After helping the children dress in new clothes that had arrived for them, Monet glanced at the clock and saw she had fifty minutes before the party. Fifty minutes to try to pull something together for herself. She returned to her room to see what she could do, and stopped short at the sight of a stunning strapless red silk ball gown hanging from the frame of her four-poster bed.

For a split second she couldn't breathe. Marcu hadn't forgotten her, either.

She blinked and tried to take another breath. It was the most beautiful dress she'd ever seen, the boned bodice and gleaming silk skirt embellished with embroidered white flowers and green beaded leaves. The skirt was cut narrow and featured a dramatic train. Monet could recognize the designer from the construction of the exquisite bodice, and the shape of the skirt. This was old-school glamour, Italian couture, a gown that probably equaled half of her annual salary. If not more.

Silk heels sat on the floor, just beneath the long silk gown, the shoes red, perfectly matching the dress.

"What on earth?" she whispered, lifting the hem of the gown to feel the luxurious fabric.

A little girl giggled behind her and Monet turned to see Rocca standing there, beaming with pleasure. "Papà bought it for you," Rocca said happily, pressing her hands to her own silk dress, the red of her gown darker, deeper, like the color of burgundy wine. "He had it flown in from Milan. It's by a famous person." She ran over to pick up one of Monet's high heels. "These match your dress, too!"

"It's incredible," Monet said, so overwhelmed she didn't know what to think.

"Do you need help dressing?" Rocca asked.

"No, my love, I'm good. Why don't you keep an eye on Antonio so he doesn't get his handsome suit dirty before everyone arrives?"

Marcu had said he'd invited everyone from the village, and everyone from the village came.

He'd also said that he'd tried to make the ballroom festive, and he'd done far, far more than that. The ballroom had been turned into a winter wonderland with a huge Christmas tree dominating the middle of the room, easily fifteen feet high, and covered in thousands of tiny white lights.

Fragrant green garlands were swagged over the doorways, and framed the tall windows. Ornate gingerbread houses filled a banquet table, the houses created by the Swiss chef who'd come to lend the Uberto cook a hand. Tables groaned beneath the weight of all the food and drink and candles. It was just as Rocca had wanted, a glittering holiday party with music and dancing and much laughter.

Entering the ballroom, Monet felt overdressed as no one else had such a formal gown, but after enough guests arrived, and the music was playing, she forgot her self-consciousness, and enjoyed watching the children play with the children from the village. Now and then Rocca would run to Monet and give her hand a squeeze. "Isn't this fun?" she'd say. "Just like in *The Nutcracker*!"

Each time Monet would squeeze her hand back, and say, "Yes. And isn't it wonderful?"

More than once her eyes would fill with tears because it really was a gorgeous party, and ev-

eryone was so happy, and this was what Marcu's life should be like—busy, warm, loving,
filled with friends and music and laughter.

Monet felt fortunate to be part of the Christmas celebration. It felt a bit like a miracle and
she would always be grateful she was here to
witness it.

During the party, Marcu couldn't keep his eyes
off Monet. She was dazzling in the red silk ball
gown, her bare shoulders gleaming, her dark
hair swept into a half-up, half-down style that
made her look like a fairy-tale princess. She
was the most beautiful woman he'd ever seen
in his life, and he loved her. All she needed was
a tiara to finish the vision. A tiara, and his ring
on her finger.

He loved her.

He'd never loved any woman but her. No
woman had ever felt so right in his arms. No
woman's kiss or touch had ever affected him
so strongly. There had been plenty of women
in his life, women he'd desired and cared for,
but no one that mattered to him like Monet.
No woman made him want to throw caution
to the wind. He'd only ever lost his head once,

and it was with her, eight years ago. And fast-forward to the present, she still had that same power over him. It didn't make sense, either. He had analyzed his actions in the past, analyzed his response to her then and now, and there was no rational answer for why he felt this want and need for her. The desire wasn't logical. There was nothing logical about the attraction, or the emotional connection between them, which was so deep he didn't know how to articulate it. Truthfully, his need for her, his desire to have her in his life, at his side, forever, was baffling if only because he couldn't find words to explain it. It simply was. And she mattered that much.

And why her?

He didn't know the answer to that, either, only that her smile gave light and life to his heart. Her eyes—so expressive—revealed so many truths, and he needed them. He needed her. He needed her honesty, and her ability to stand up to him, and confront him when he was wrong. So many people tried to impress him, and court his favor, but she wasn't one of them. She never had been.

* * *

The guests were all gone. The children had been taken to bed and would be tucked in by Elise while the rest of the staff moved through the *castello*, blowing out candles, extinguishing lights, locking doors in all rooms but the ballroom as Marcu had given them instructions to leave the ballroom alone. And now Marcu had Monet alone. His heart pounded and he felt like a boy—shy, nervous, ridiculously tongue-tied—as he drew Monet closer to the soaring Christmas tree, still glittering with lights and delicate glass ornaments, and the beautiful hand-carved angels.

"It was a beautiful party," Monet said.

"It was."

"I think everyone had an incredible time," she added, as they gazed up at the tree.

"Yes."

"I've never been so surprised," she said, glancing at him with a smile. "Who knew that Marcu Uberto, who doesn't celebrate Christmas, would throw the most magical Christmas party I've ever been to?"

"It was Rocca's idea," he answered, pulse thudding.

"Rocca is an incredible little girl."

"She is," he agreed, before drawing a deep breath. "And you are an incredible woman. I don't know how you've done it, but you've changed everything in a matter of days. You arrived here nine days ago and somehow saved all of us."

"Not so."

"It is so." His voice dropped, deepening with emotion, emotion that filled his chest with warmth. "I'm so grateful to you, Monet, for so many things, but maybe I'm most grateful for your love, and your faith in me. Even when you're angry with me, you still somehow believe in me, and that has made all the difference."

He reached into his pocket and pulled out the delicate gold ring with the two-carat ruby he'd bought for her ten years ago, when she'd turned sixteen. "This is temporary," he said, rolling the ring between his fingers. "Just until I can get you the perfect, forever ring, but I've held on to this all these years, and it's my promise to you, that I will always take care of you, and love you, for the rest of our lives." And then he kneeled down, in front of her, and reached for her hand. "Monet, would you please marry me? I love you, and I can't imagine my life without you."

Monet stood frozen in shock as Marcu slid her ruby ring on her finger, specifically on her ring finger on her left hand.

It was a ring she hadn't seen in eight years. He'd given it to her for her sixteenth birthday, but she'd chosen to leave it behind when she'd left Palermo.

Monet's mouth dried and she struggled to speak, but words wouldn't come and her emotions were beyond chaotic, flooding her with shock and then grief, because she couldn't say yes to him, she couldn't. "Marcu, please," she whispered, tugging on his hand. "Please get up. Please stand."

"You haven't answered me," he said.

"Because I can't answer you. You don't really love me."

"I do. Very much."

She shook her head, and struggled to get the ring off her finger. "How can you? You don't even know me—"

"You are smart, and kind, as well as fiercely loyal," he interrupted, rising, and yet he remained close. "You wouldn't be here now if you weren't. But you're also independent and demand respect, and I do respect you, very much, and I want what's best for you."

"And you think you are what's best for me?" she asked, voice strangled, still frantically trying to get the ring off, and yet it seemed stuck, already.

"I think I could be. With your help." His voice deepened. "I'm not without flaws, and I need to work on things, but with you, I can be the man you deserve—"

"Marcu, stop. Please stop. This is too painful, *please.*" Her eyes shimmered with tears and she knocked them away, giving up on the ring to fight the tears. "You will forget me as soon as I go. You will move on quickly. It's what you do, and who you are—"

"Because I married Galeta?"

"Yes! Within months of me leaving. And you didn't come find me, and you didn't try to reach out to me. You just dropped me at the airport and we were done, and that's not love. Nor have you changed. You're here because Vittoria was on the other side of the mountain—"

"Not true. Not even close to being true."

"So you didn't marry Galeta months after I left?"

"Yes, I did. I'd gotten her pregnant and she was a good person. I'd known her forever, since we were children. She left to go to boarding school right around the time you and your mother arrived in Palermo. I didn't see her again for years, but she was easy to like. You would have liked her—"

"I doubt that!"

"No, you would have. She wasn't your typical heiress. She was the opposite of a socialite. Galeta didn't enjoy public attention or the spotlight. In fact our biggest source of tension was the media, and controlling the paparazzi. She was as livid as I was that our wedding was in the tabloids. We'd both wanted a private wedding and she wondered who'd sneaked all those personal photos to them and demanded I investigate and fire those who had betrayed our trust."

"Did you investigate?"

"Yes."

"Who was it?"

"It was my father. He leaked his own son's

wedding photos, wanting you to know I was married, and no longer available."

"He loved my mother but despised me."

"He didn't despise you, but he was old-fashioned in that he wanted a Sicilian daughter-in-law, so that his grandchildren would be Sicilian." He shrugged impatiently. "I don't blame him, though. I blame myself. He didn't fail you. I did. I should have gone after you. I should have protected you. I should have been the man you needed."

"I was just eighteen, and not ready to marry. Everything worked out the way it was meant to work out." She took a panicked step backward, feeling foolish in the stunning ball gown. She'd been overdressed from the start. She wasn't a princess. She wasn't even Cinderella. She was nothing...nothing at all...and she just wanted to go home now. She wanted to return to London more than she'd ever wanted anything. "I'm sorry to disappoint you, but I must leave first thing in the morning. I want to leave quickly, quietly, without fuss."

He said nothing.

"You promised me," she said, voice trembling. "You promised me—"

"I'll take you to the helicopter," he said flatly, cutting her short. "It's still here. I'll make sure you're on it early in the morning."

"And the rest of the way? You'll get me a ticket home?"

"My plane will be fueled in Milan, waiting for you."

She nodded, and glanced down at the ring on her finger. The band was delicate and elegant, and then there was the rich red ruby gleaming in the middle. "Twice you've given this to me," she said, once again trying to tug it off, "and now twice I give it back to you—"

"No." He caught her hand, and pushed the ring back down. "It's yours. It was something I had made for you for your sixteenth birthday. It's yours, and I ask you to take it with you. Once you're in London you can do what you want with it, but please don't leave it here. I've held on to it all these years, but I can't do it anymore."

She nodded again and then glanced at the tree, with the lights and beautiful decorations, and then at him, so still, so hurt, so proud, and blinking back tears, she hurried from the ballroom.

* * *

Monet couldn't get out of the ball gown fast enough, and she scrubbed the makeup off her face, before splashing cold water over it to stop the tears.

She couldn't cry.

She couldn't think.

She couldn't feel.

Just go to bed. Just get through the next eight hours and she'd be gone. Away. Free.

Monet crawled into bed, shivering. She buried her face in the pillow, trying to hold the emotion in.

Marcu had proposed to her...he'd gotten down on one knee and asked her to be his wife, and he'd said the words she'd longed to hear but she didn't believe them, which was why she couldn't accept the proposal.

She finally broke down, and cried, hard, before falling asleep, but she couldn't stay asleep, tossing and turning all night, until she left the bed and went to sit in a chair by the window, wrapped in her duvet, and watched the sun rise over the mountain, painting the white valley floor pink and gold.

She didn't think she'd ever seen such a beautiful sunrise. She tried to drink it in, despite the fact that her eyes were dry and gritty from too little sleep.

Out there somewhere was the helicopter waiting for her. Marcu had said he'd make the necessary travel arrangements and she knew he would.

Once the sun was all the way up, she made a pot of tea and focused on packing, determined to leave before the children woke. She left the ball gown and shoes that had arrived via helicopter yesterday in the wardrobe. She would never wear them again, nor did she want to take them back to London with her. They'd just serve as a painful reminder of her time here.

Bags packed, Monet straightened her room, returned a damp towel to the en-suite bathroom, put away the teakettle and began to make the bed. They were silly tasks but tidying her room gave her a sense of closure.

"What are you doing?" Marcu's deep voice sounded, startling her.

She hadn't heard her outer door open, and she jerked upright, pulse pounding. She hadn't seen him, or spoken to him, since she'd gone to bed last night. "Making the bed," she answered, forcing herself back to action, smoothing the bottom sheet before drawing up the duvet.

"Before you leave?"

"I can't leave a messy room."

"We have staff here," he said, approaching. "You're not a maid."

"I'm more comfortable doing it myself. I grew up this way." She glanced at him, trying to keep her pulse steady, not easy when he stood impossibly close to her, and the bed. He looked grim, and tired. She suspected he hadn't slept very well last night, either. But she couldn't dwell on that.

"We had staff and help at the palazzo," he said.

"Yes, you did, but my mother and I took care of our own rooms, and we always did our own beds. The staff would wash our sheets and return them folded, but we did everything else."

"I had no idea."

"My mother worried that the staff would think less of us if we put on airs." She managed a tight smile. "She might have been your father's mistress, but she never forgot she was just another member of his staff."

"Monet!"

His sharp tone drew tears to her eyes. She curled her fingers into a ball, feeling the press of the ruby ring. She hadn't taken it off. It was her own ring after all, given to her by him years ago. At the very least, she could leave with it. "It's how she felt," she said quietly, defensively. "I'm sorry if it hurts."

"I don't think you're sorry it hurts. I think you want to hurt me now. You want to draw blood because you're refusing what you want—"

"That's ludicrous!"

"You love me. I know you do. I know you have always loved me, just as I have always loved you, but because I haven't expressed my love correctly, properly, to your standards, it's not enough."

"That's not true."

"No? Then why refuse me? Why not give me a chance?"

Her mouth opened, and then closed without making a sound because she didn't have an answer for him. She didn't know why she couldn't consider his proposal. She just couldn't…there wasn't enough trust left inside her. "I'm all ready to go," she said. "I just have those bags there."

His gaze swept the room, stopping on the wardrobe with the open door. Her red ball gown was on a hanger inside. "I'll take your bags," he said curtly.

"I'll meet you downstairs."

Marcu tried not to think as he drove Monet to the helipad in the valley. His chest felt bruised, as if he'd taken a hard blow on the left side and he kept having to hold his breath to keep the pain at bay.

He felt as if he was in Palermo driving her to the airport eight years ago. He'd hated that day, and he hated this one. The last thing he wanted was for her to leave, but he had made her a promise that when she asked to leave, he would let her go. He was letting her go.

As he pulled up to the gates he could see his helicopter and pilots waiting. He ground his teeth together. His chest was already on fire and pain filled him, making every nerve and muscle hurt.

He loved her and she didn't believe him. He loved her and had tried to show her, organizing a festive party to demonstrate that he would try to be a better man. That he was willing to change. That indeed he was already changed.

He didn't need her for the children. The children were actually fine. They had a kind, devoted nanny who'd return soon from England, and they had a father who loved them.

He was the one who needed her. He was the one whose life had never been the same after she'd left Palermo, and now she was leaving again. Leaving him again. And it burned within him, the pain and the need and the disappointment with himself for not being able to convince her.

He slowed, and then shifted into Park, as they arrived on the tarmac.

He hated to let her go. He hated that he had failed her not once, but twice. For a moment Marcu felt sick, nauseated by the past, and then he made a deliberate decision to let the past and the painful emotion go. He wasn't who he'd been, and even though this was ending just as badly as it had in Palermo, he knew without a doubt this time that he loved her, and that there would never be anyone for him but her.

Monet didn't just own his heart. She was his heart.

CHAPTER ELEVEN

SHE WAS BACK at work for the huge sales going on after Christmas, sales that continued into the New Year, and through the second week of January. During the week the store was less frantic, but on weekends the traffic always picked up and today was no exception.

Monet was grateful that work had been so busy because it kept her from thinking too much, and prevented her from falling apart. Every day she questioned her decision to reject Marcu's proposal. Every day she kicked herself, angry that she'd been so quick to refuse him instead of asking for more time.

She'd been proud and stubborn, impulsive and frightened, and she had just possibly destroyed her last chance for true love, and happiness.

Maybe if the time she'd spent with Marcu had been different. Maybe if it hadn't been such a whirlwind trip she could have been more ob-

jective. Instead she'd felt swept into an Alpine
fantasy, complete with adorable children and
a handsome profoundly sexy bachelor father,
with snow and snow and more snow, as well
as that glorious Christmas proposal before the
towering Christmas tree in the ballroom—and
it was fantastic and impossible. It was fiction,
just like *The Nutcracker* that Monet had read
to Rocca every day.

And so she'd turned Marcu down to make
a point—she was fine, she was strong—but
Monet feared she'd cut off her nose to spite
her face.

Marcu wasn't prone to grand romantic gestures but he'd tried that Christmas night. He'd
organized the party and sent everyone away so
he could propose before the tree. It had been
romantic, and she'd been wearing a perfect
princess gown, but she wasn't a princess. She'd
never be a princess.

Monet's eyes grew hot and gritty and a lump
filled her throat. She was so upset that her hands
shook as she adjusted the delicate lace wedding
gown hanging next to the cash register. She had
to keep it together. There would be no breaking
down at work. Which was why she couldn't let

herself think of him anymore. Easier said than done when everything in her missed him and had loved being with Marcu and his children. He did feel like home. He was the only home she'd ever known and she'd given it all up again because she had to be strong. She had to be—

She turned at the sound of a violin, recognizing the first haunting notes, but not yet certain it was what she thought the song might be. And then as a voice began to sing, shivers coursed up and down her spine.

Puccini's *Gianni Schicchi*. Her favorite opera.

Voice after voice joined in. But was the song playing though the department's speaker? Or was there a performance taking place in the store?

She crossed the marble floor and discovered the musicians were on her floor, seated in folding chairs in front of the big arched window.

Stringed instruments, a harp, wind instruments—the musicians were filling in from the sides.

A woman stepped toward her, singing. It was the woman she'd just spoken to fifteen minutes ago, about mother-of-the-bride gowns. Monet's mouth dropped open as she realized that half the people singing and playing instruments had been customers moments ago, or had at least been pretending to be customers...

And these "customers" weren't just singing any song, but *"E Lui,"* in which Gianni Schicchi refused to allow his daughter, Lauretta, to marry her boyfriend, Rinuccio, and everyone was fighting and arguing and the couple was distraught.

Monet's heart pounded as music soared, and the superb voices rose, overlapping, echoing off the ceiling, and filled the high domed ceiling of the fifth floor.

Monet had used to attend the opera in Palermo with the Ubertos, and this had been her favorite. She'd spent hours listening to the recording in Marcu's room, playing her favorite aria, *"O Mio Babbino Caro,"* over and over.

As *"E Lui"* ended there was a beat of silence before a lovely young woman in a red dress—the bride Monet had been helping earlier—began to sing, the lyrics so familiar to Monet, with Lauretta pleading with her father to let her marry her beloved because she couldn't live without him.

Every great soprano had sung *"O Mio Babbino Caro,"* and Monet was moved to tears.

Lauretta was poor. She couldn't marry her Rinuccio because she had no dowry. And yet she loved Rinuccio so much that she told her father she'd die without him…

The heart-rending aria filled the great glass dome with sound, the acoustics perfect, and Monet cried harder, wiping away tears but unable to catch them all.

Only one person knew how much she loved this opera and this aria. Only one person knew she'd once compared herself to Lauretta, a girl from humble origins who'd never be accepted by her beloved's wealthy family as she came without a dowry…

As the soprano reached the end, the fifth floor was overflowing with people, the crowd spilling off the escalators and out of the elevators to watch, and listen. Then it was over, and there was a moment of rapt silence before thunderous applause.

Monet clapped, and tried to dry her eyes, but she was a mess. This had to be Marcu's doing. It had to be, but where was he?

And then he was there, walking through the

crowd, sophisticated and dashing in a black suit and black shirt, the shirt open at the throat, revealing his lovely lightly tanned skin. His gaze met hers and held as he approached, and she didn't know what to think or feel, not when she was already feeling so much, undone by the music and the memories and the past that she couldn't ever seem to come to grips with, even though she'd tried. How she'd tried.

"What have you done?" she choked, as he crossed to her, and took her hand. "Have you seen all these people?"

"Yes."

"This was crazy. I'm shaking."

He put an arm around her and pulled her close. "You loved that aria, remember?"

Fresh tears filled her eyes and she couldn't speak, and so she nodded her head. "Why?" she whispered when she could.

"I needed to get your attention. I hope I have."

She cried harder, and she didn't know why she was crying, only that it felt so good to be in his arms. She'd missed him so much. Too much. It had been awful these past few weeks and she'd wanted to go to him so many times.

"How did you manage this?" she said, cheek pressed to his chest.

"Not easily. Hit a few roadblocks until I reached out to the English National Opera."

She laughed and blinked back tears. "It's incredible, but also not private."

"Not at all private. Some might say it's a spectacle."

"Indeed. You've put on quite a show, *signor*."

"I'm not finished, either," he said, taking a ring box from his pocket and kneeling in front of her. "I want the world to know I love you, and have only ever loved you, and I will spend the rest of my life trying to make it up to you—"

She reached down and clasped his hands. "You don't have to do this here, and you don't have to say these things—"

"But I do, because I love you, and I'm once again asking you to marry me, not because I need a wife, but because I need *you*, and only you, and if you're not ready to accept me now, then I'll wait, and I'll ask you again in six months, and then again in another six months."

Monet straightened and clasped her hands together, pulse pounding.

He looked up at her, his expression serious, his light blue eyes intently holding her gaze. "If you say you need six years, I'll give you that, too, but there will never be anyone else for me. It is you, and only you." He opened the ring box to reveal a stunning emerald cut diamond—that was huge, easily three or four carats in size—with smaller baguette diamonds on either side. "I will wait for you, because I love you, and life isn't complete without you. In fact, life isn't even life without you."

She glanced from the ring to his face. "I do love you," she whispered. "Very, very much. But I'm scared—"

"I know."

"I've been alone for so much of my life."

"I know that, too."

"I don't trust easily."

The corner of his mouth lifted. "Yes."

"But I can't imagine life without you. I don't want to do this without you anymore." She flexed her left hand, where she still wore her sixteenth-birthday ring. "I haven't taken this off, because it's been my last connection to you."

"Ring, or no ring, I'm not going anywhere."

"We can wait on setting a wedding date?"

"As long as you want."

She smiled. "Then, yes. I accept your proposal. Yes."

He stood and slipped her birthday ring off, and put it on her right hand, before sliding the engagement ring onto her finger, and then he kissed her, a long searing kiss filled with heat and love, as the crowd applauded, and someone whistled, the sound echoing off the domed ceiling with its incredible acoustics.

EPILOGUE

SHE DIDN'T NEED six years or even six months to know she wanted to marry him. They decided to continue working and then spend weekends together, and after just a month of Marcu bringing the children to London to see her, followed by her traveling to Sicily to see them, she knew the sooner they came together as a family, the better. The children did need her and so did Marcu, who worried more and slept less when she was in London on her own.

The wedding took place the first weekend in June at the great cathedral in Palermo, the one the family had always attended. The weather was perfect for a wedding, too, the sky a stunning azure-blue with just a few wispy clouds overhead. It was warm but not too warm and the cathedral's bells rang joyfully as Monet and Marcu stepped from the cool interior into the glorious sunshine, her hand tucked in the crook of Marcu's arm.

Man and wife.

Married.

She looked up at him, and he smiled his dazzling heart-stopping smile, before his head dropped and he kissed her thoroughly, making her tingle from head to toe. *"La mia adorabile moglie,"* he said huskily. My lovely wife.

She couldn't hide her blush, or her smile, as he lifted his head. Wife. She was his wife.

The children came running toward them then, Matteo, Rocca, and Antonio, all throwing themselves at the bridal couple, and there were hugs all around.

"I love you," Monet said, kissing each of the children, one by one. "You are mine now, forever and ever."

"And you four are all mine," Marcu said, wrapping an arm around her waist. "I have everything now, love and family. I am, without a doubt, the luckiest of men."

* * * * *